DEDICATED TO MY SON JELANI AMARE WILLIS (R.I.P)

02/17/2021-12/30/2021

We love you dearly and you will always be in our hearts.

-Dad.

TABLE OF CONTENTS

Prologue: The Forbidden Plan

It is a dark and rainy night, of course all good stories start off that way right, and two government figures stand in the dark walkway under the bridge in the city park. One of them lights a cigarette, "he's late!" As he exhales the smoke into the agent's face. "Who does he think I am?" Suddenly the sounds of approaching footsteps as a third figure begins to emerge from the moonlit shadows. "What took you so long? I have been down here for an hour now; do you want this or not?" He throws his cigarette on the ground and stomps it, exhales the smoke, and reaches inside of his coat and pulls out a government file. "I am the secretary general of the assembled states" said the approaching figure, "do not ever question me, do you know how hard it is to get a moment of privacy." "I hope this is worth my time, you should be glad I am helping you Mr. Director. Now let us see what you have." The director of operations hands the files to the secretary general. "Yes sir, here you are" replied the director of operations as he reached for another cigarette. "don't smoke those things around me" said the secretary general "and who is he?" A third figure steps forward "honorable secretary general, I am agent Samuel, it was I who initiated the G.A.M.E program. I developed its technologies and training programs, not only that, but I am its first agent myself. I have learned how to synthesize the waters of the green pond and unlock its hidden potentials giving a normal human the ability to advance forward in their evolutionary status and therefore gaining extraordinary abilities." said Samuel. "Impressive, tell me how" said the secretary general. Samuel smiled "**water memory** is the ability of **water** to retain a **memory** of substances previously dissolved in it even after an arbitrary number of serial dilutions. The **water memory theory** defies conventional scientific understanding of physical chemistry knowledge, and the water memory theory has not been accepted by the scientific community, but this does not mean that it is not true. I studied this and to see how far back in time I could find the origins of the unique green color of this water." Samuel continued. "By creating multiple copies of itself life survives, everything can do this, this process is replicating or reproducing. All DNA hold information about past copies and future copies." The secretary began to grow annoyed "what's your point Samuel, I do not have all night for a bedtime story" Samuel smiled "what I am trying to say sir is that we were able to trace this water back to the time when the gods were on earth. This spring, the green pond was the water that they drank and used. The waters' powers are lying doormat and untapped. Everything that encounters this water changes them." The secretary general begins to smile "this all sounds too good to be true." The director of operations steps forward with a serious look on his face. "Please sir, let him finish, there is something you need to know" the secretary general looked at Samuel, he was still smiling. "Samuel" said the secretary general, Samuel continued, "scientific studies have shown that water, not only has memory but water's structure is changed by the emotions of people. The water molecules change their position when they interact with positive or negative emotions. The structure of water is more important than its composition…" the director of operations interrupted "…sir, we have created mutants! Once we discovered what the water could do, we assessed it on Samuel and the results were amazing, so we began to mass produce a spray from the water, giving it to soldiers. We soon started to discover that the results affected everyone differently and the number of mutations began to grow larger than the successful ones. We called in a private scientist to study the water around the clock to find a solution, but no solution emerged.

I ordered the operation to be shut down it was not too late to clean up our tracks, but the information leaked and there was a riot. Looters destroyed the labs, and all the chemicals were thrown into the green pond. Now the entire pond is contaminated, and the waters are unstable. For the pursuit of power people have been sacrificing themselves to see if they will be blessed or cursed so we have had to build a barrier around the water and we must have the military guarding it, we need the assistance of the assembled states." Samuel was still smiling as the director explained this to the secretary general. "He doesn't seem so worried" said the secretary general. "That's because of the G.A.M.E. Program that he created," said the director. "He created a government organization that recruits the best officers, soldiers, and enhanced persons to help defend against the growing number of mutants. We have already been tracking them since this thing begin and we arc still working to perfect the formula to create more soldiers." The director continued "we need the assembled states to contain this information from the other nations, provide backup military support if we need it and grant us scientist and funding. Can you imagine if this thing gets to the rest of the world?" This is the first time that Samuel stopped smiling and the secretary general noticed it. "Director, can you give me and Samuel time to talk about this. I promise your city will have the full support of the assembled states, but we will have access to the green pond water, and I want all scientific results." The director nods his head and walks off "yes sir." Samuel and the secretary general wait until they are alone. "Is he gone" stated the secretary general. "Yes, we are alone." Said Samuel as he begins to show his true form. Although appearing as human Samuel is much more. He is an entity from another dimension manifesting on this planet. During ancient times he was known as a messenger from the kingdom of light. An Angel "Are you sure this is going to work?" said the secretary general as he began to reveal his true appearance. Another entity from the same dimension as Samuel but his energy signature is much more cynical and misanthropically relayed, during ancient times he was known as a demon. "Yes, the humans are not aware" said Samuel "I still hate they were even created; we must stay under the radar for now so that heavens do not realize anything until we are ready. Prepare your demons and your generals. If we are discovered, I am sure the prince of light will send his precious archangels to protect humanity, we do not stand a chance against the archangels now." The demon smiled, "maybe I can convince my father to ask the horsemen to help us out" Samuel shook his head. "No, I don't want the horsemen involved, I don't want the archangels involved and I definitely do not want the prince of darkness or the prince of light to know anything." I want humans to destroy themselves, we have planted the seeds of hatred, power, corruption, pride, and fear. Our time will come to reveal ourselves to regain our rightful place. No angel should be forced to serve these insignificant weak creatures" Samuel looks at the demon with fire in his eyes. "I hope I can trust you demon, although I hate humans, I still do not take a demon for granted. Especially Gorax, younger brother to the Grim spook and the three demon sons of the dark prince. Gorax smiles, "you are a very observant angel, I did not think you would recognize me. The heavens are preparing." Samuel turns to walk away "I am helping you demon, but I am loyal to my angels. Once the humans are out of the way the war will begin again and I will do what I must to protect the heavens. We are not friend's Gorax; remember that should you ever cross me." Gorax smiles in arrogance. "Just do your job Samuel and when this is all over, I would love to rip those annoying wings from you and give them to my father as a gift. Remember that if you decide to cross me." Samuel shrugs it off and begins to fly away. "I suggest you read the file demon, with the help of the green god water humans are just as strong if not stronger than demons and angels. These are your greatest threats. I am handing them to you on a silver platter. Eliminate the human elites, they have the blood of the gods, and they can be problems. Once the enhanced elites are destroyed the rest of humanity will not pose a threat. I will do what I can from the inside." Samuel flies away. Gorax changes his form back to the secretary general and begins walking back to his car. "Humans stronger than demons" he thinks to himself in laughter as he enters his car. "Drive me home" the secretary general says as he begins to read the files and the collection of information given to him by the angel. Let us see what these humans are up to this time, I will impress father first and I am sure he will grant me greater power than my brothers. I want to be the next dark lord and I am going to prove it by destroying all of humanity and the angels at the same time.

Sponsored by 1031 Productions

G.A.M.E Profiles & Logs
(Green Pond City Government Files)

<u>**Green Pond Background:**</u>

Green Pond City was always a city of great economic profits due to its scientific and military advancements. **Green Pond City** is located within the land of "**Moselle.**" We are the center land of the five Great Sovereign Nations of the world. The land of "**Arunika**" is to the north. There you will find the **city of the Sun** and its **dynasties.** To the south is the land of "**Demetria**" and **Arctic city** with its **villages**. On our east side is the land of "**Zion**" and the **tribes** of the **primeval forest**, finally on our west side is "**Terran**" and the **underground colonies** of **Hypogean**. Green Pond City and its **citizens** are very wealthy, and they have many enemies. The current government came into power with the discovery of the mysterious green pond in the center of the city. As beautiful as the water was it wasn't consumable and usually made people sick. Organizations of people came together to protect and study the water, eventually those people became the government. Over the years there were many studies, and the government grew but answers about green water were never revealed to the people of the city. Eventually many people forgot about the water. Although the government never stopped its studies, no one ever imagined they would discover the source of the water.

<u>**Green Pond City's history: The emergence of power.**</u>

The year the discovery was made that the Green Pond City water unlocked special abilities and true powers for certain people that consumed or were exposed to the mysterious element in the water. The water flows naturally from a spring in the middle of the city. A select few special, and extra ordinary citizens partnered with the government to protect, store and properly dispose of the toxic water. Initially the government was overrun by groups of rouge citizen as they overtook the government facilities and claimed this special water for themselves, not understanding its power, thousands of ordinary citizens interacted with the water and quickly begin mutating. To some the water was a gift to others a curse as Green Pond City was quickly overrun. The government recruited some of the citizens for themselves to help defend and take back control of this invaluable resource and maintain proper control of its distribution. Mutations or civilians caught with power will be subject to the judicial systems, courts, police and enforcement. **The G.A.M.E" the Guardians Against Mutation Enhancement** is the governing program authorized to handle these threats.

<u>**Special Ability Categories:**</u>
Mutations (enhancements gone wrong)

Enhanced abilities, a perfect bonding to the human body increases some natural abilities.

Enhanced Externals- No natural special abilities, abilities come from enchanted or enhanced material.

Mystics, usually using summoning's and channeling They use the power of nature, spiritual beings, to aid them. Ultimately mystics are servants for their abilities.

Vigilantes: Ordinary humans with nothing more than will power and intelligence, Vigilantes, considered civilians by some, only use the tools of mankind to enhance or augment their abilities, some tools have been able to even compete with the **Enhanced Externals.**

Semi-Gods- Usually thought to have divine power, these extremely powerful nearly immortals are either cursed, servants of the GODS, or Demi Gods themselves. They seem to be hidden among us all the time.

GODS- These very rare, almost never seen beings are sometimes worshipped by the civilian's and feared by all. Their powers are beyond imagination sometimes, but they can only manipulate so much energy before they are forced into a deep sleep to recharge. Usually responsible for creating and manipulating realities to their wills. They are the origins of energy manipulation and power.

End of Document

Table of Documented Abilities and Special interest Profiles

1. Awesome Man- Greg Williams (E.E)

2. Nuclear Man- John Wagner (E.E)

3. Black night-Damion Johnson (Vig)

4. Stalker-Marcus Williams (enhanced abilities)

5. The Great Phantom- Josh Williams (E.E) (Mys)

6. Madam Cat-Angela McWaters (muta)

7. ██████████-Classified

8. Soundwave-Leyla Jones (vig)

9. Star- Issa -(mut)

10. Cyber-Alex Cabe (E.E)

11. Axel Blaze-Axel Summers (E.E)

12. ██████████Classified

13. ██████████████Classified

14. ██████████████Classified

15. White Wolf-Jimmy brewer (Enhanced Abilities)

16. ████████████████████Classified

17. ██████████████Classified

18. ██████████████Classified

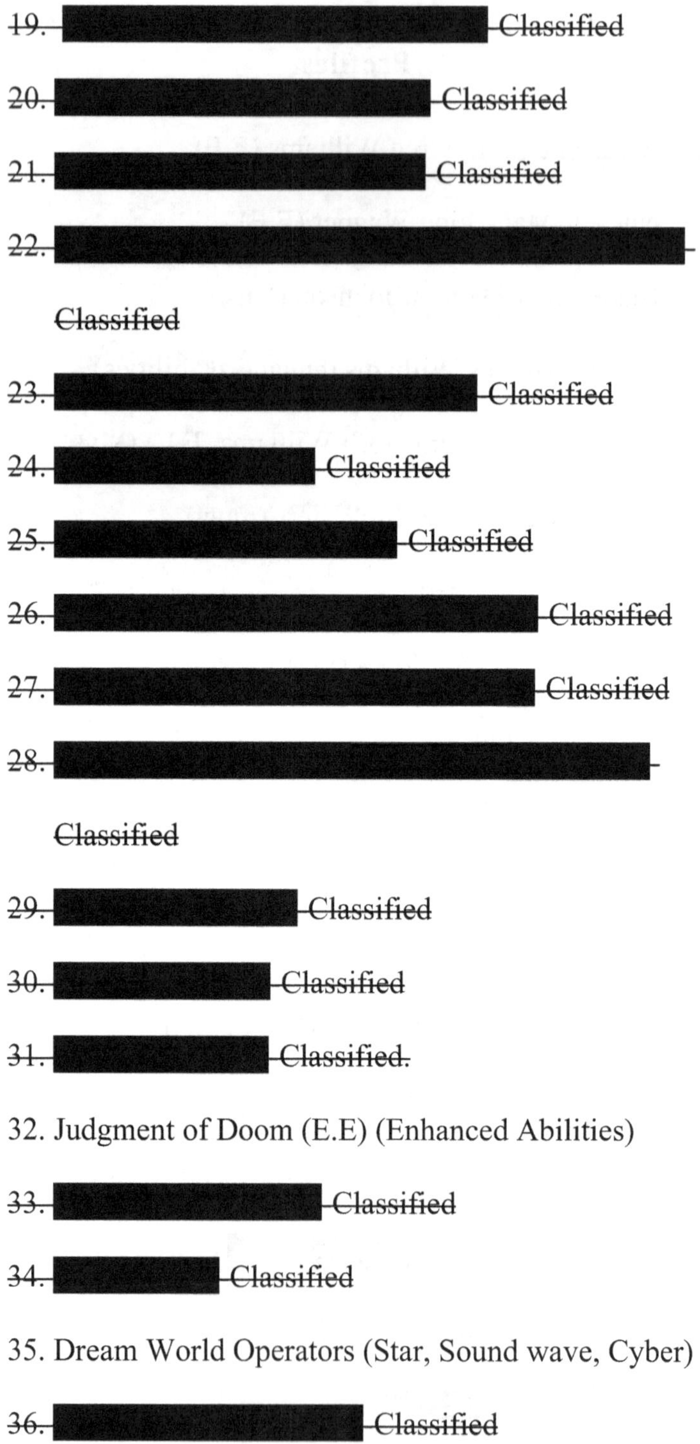

19. Classified

20. Classified

21. Classified

22.

Classified

23. Classified

24. Classified

25. Classified

26. Classified

27. Classified

28.

Classified

29. Classified

30. Classified

31. Classified.

32. Judgment of Doom (E.E) (Enhanced Abilities)

33. Classified

34. Classified

35. Dream World Operators (Star, Sound wave, Cyber)

36. Classified

37. ~~Classified~~

38. Canine (Mut)

39. Cindy Young/ Greg's Girlfriend/Awesome girl

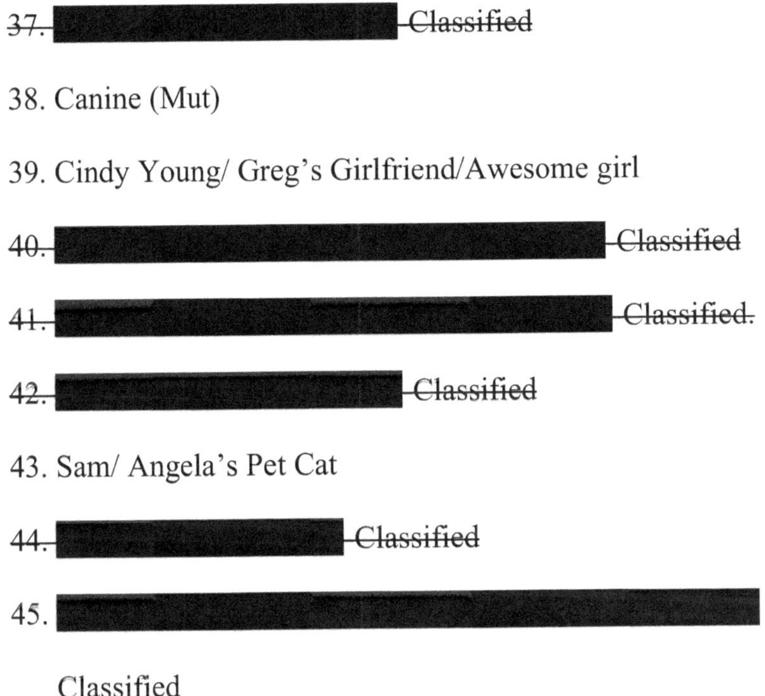

40. ~~Classified~~

41. ~~Classified.~~

42. ~~Classified~~

43. Sam/ Angela's Pet Cat

44. ~~Classified~~

45.

Classified

Public Name: THE AWESOME MAN
Real Name: Dr. Greg Williams
Birthdate: January 13
Age: 24
Height 5'9
Weight:187
Eyes: Blue
Hair: Blonde
Race: Human
Occupation: Chemist

What Chemists and Materials Scientists Do

Chemists and materials scientists study substances at the atomic and molecular levels and the ways in which the substances interact with one another. They use their knowledge to develop new and improved products and to test the quality of manufactured goods.

Work Environment

Chemists and materials scientists work in laboratories and offices. They typically work full-time and keep regular hours.

<u>**How to Become a Chemist or Materials Scientist**</u>
Chemists and materials scientists need at least a bachelor's degree in chemistry or a related field. However, a master's degree or Ph.D. is needed for many research jobs.
<u>**Pay**</u>
The median annual wage for chemists and materials scientists was $72,610 in May 2015.

Background: Dr. Greg Williams was the youngest graduate in his university studying chemistry and biology he graduated as a Biochemist working for Green Pond City. Greg's Family, the Williams were always agents for the city, and he followed his parent's career path to work for the government and help develop and maintain the city. He was unaware of the secret projects and other developments that his father helped to create and how involved his family name is with many secret government projects. During the events surrounding the "emergence of power" and the mutant infestation of the city, his family was targeted for assassination to cover evidence of the government involvement in the infestation. Greg begins to discover the true reason he and his family were targeted when he finds a secret government weapon hidden in his home. He uses that weapon to investigate what happened to his family, but what he finds is more than he could imagine.

Description of powers: Greg's powers come from the mysterious gloves he wears; they reflect his determination, and they produce a power like electricity. He can release small or large blast of electricity that usually weaken his enemy but depending on his emotional stability and mood these electrical charged could easily kill. He has the ability to levitate using electro-magnetism His abilities are limited to his individual ideas and thoughts of what he chooses to do with them We have only a few documented sightings of his abilities used in minor battles but we have yet to see Dr. Williams Release his abilities on a large scale from our calculations His abilities, If overloaded, could probably create a destructive blast of electricity that could disintegrate anything within **135.4 mi²** reaching temperatures as hot as the surface of the sun.

List of Known Abilities: Lightning is one of the most beautiful displays in nature. It is also one of the deadliest natural phenomena known to man. With bolt temperatures, hotter than the surface of the sun and shockwaves beaming out in all directions, lightning is a lesson in physical science and humility. When the local electric field exceeds the strength of damp air (about 3 million volts per meter), electrical discharge results in a *strike*, often followed by commensurate discharges branching from the same path. Mechanisms that cause the charges to build up to lightning are still a matter of scientific investigation. Light travels at about 300,000,000 m/s, and sound travels through air at about 340 m/s

1) **The Electric Net-** The opponent is trapped inside a net of electricity that paralyzes or renders un-consciences making it easier to subdue and capture or further continue an attack and combo. The nets are usually charged before being deployed and can be delayed for a little until they are deployed it seems, but during this time you can see him charging.

2) **The Electric Wave-** It seems that during combat sometimes he can combine his attacks with electrical shockwaves that travel through the air on storm clouds. Because the electrostatic discharge of terrestrial lightning superheats the air to plasma temperatures along the length of the discharge channel in a short duration, kinetic theory dictates gaseous molecules undergo a rapid increase in

pressure and thus expand outward from the lightning creating a shock wave audible as thunder.

3) **The Electric Shield-** Mainly used as a defense Dr. Williams can either deflect or disintegrate objects and elements fired or thrown at him with tight clusters of controlled lightning strikes and deflective electromagnetism to repel. The shield is always usually an invisible field of magnetism, but he adds the electric elements as a counter measure.

4) **(Unseen) Electric Destruction-** The feared release of Dr. Williams full power in one discharge. The combined attack of an enormously growing storm cloud with the repulsive force of electro-magnetism. For a combined distance of estimated 135.4 mi^2 with temperatures reaching the surface of the sun, Average surface temperature 9,900°F (5,500°C) If he ever launces this attack, the results would permanently scar the planet's surface. The attack, however, should be very slow, to build that much force and to cover an area so large it would take nearly an hour to fully deploy and reach full destructive power. I don't see why he must use such a move or how effective it could be. With the time it takes to build up this would truly be a move used in desperation.

Public Name: The Black-Night
Real Name: Damion Johnson
Birthdate: October 25th
Age:36
Height: 6'1
Eyes: Brown, Black in tribal gear
Hair: None
Race: Human
Occupation: engineer/ Inventor

What Mechanical Engineers Do

Mechanical engineering is one of the broadest engineering disciplines. Mechanical engineers design, develop, build, and test mechanical and thermal sensors and devices, including tools, engines, and machines.

Work Environment

Mechanical engineers generally work in offices. They may occasionally visit worksites where a problem or piece of equipment needs their personal attention. Mechanical engineers work mostly in engineering services, research and development, and manufacturing.

How to Become a Mechanical Engineer

Mechanical engineers typically need a bachelor's degree in mechanical engineering or mechanical engineering technology.

Pay

The median annual wage for mechanical engineers was $83,590 in May 2015.

Background: Damion Johnson was an extremely brilliant man, even at a young age he would stand out among other students in intelligence. As a Mechanical engineer, he traveled to Moselle to becoming a famous inventor, but that vision never became a reality for him, he was called back home to face a family issue and he got caught up in gang war, he quit his career and focused full time on building his intelligence and fighting ability and decided to take his revenge out on the gang members themselves. He trained in some sort of boxing, and he has shown signs and knowledge of advanced judo skills as well. The real strength behind Damion is his Brain, he can solve almost any problem and his inventions truly are amazing, but he never wanted riches for some reason. He fights with his gadgets, using hand to hand combat as a last resort.

Description of Powers: Damion Doesn't have any powers himself besides his intellect and physical abilities, but those are usually enough. He can invent almost anything from anything else. He's able to see, analyze, and recreate a material substance within a matter of minutes in his mind and within days if given time to create a real version of what he sees. His Costume is tribal Armor given to him from his ancestors' people and its material is unknown but seems very durable. On board the computer is built into the mask and hood. Many weapons are generally used to render the opponent unconscious and they aren't very deadly to the opponent. The most interesting skill we have on record is his manipulation of light molecules and basically his ability to bend light. He has the uncanny ability to create pure darkness even in broad daylight with a distance up to a 20-mile radius.

List of Known Abilities: Damion's form of hand-to-hand combat is an ancient form of boxing from his tribal people, and he learn the customs of Japanese fighting during his time as an engineer and his travels to different lands. But your first problem is getting past his gadgets.

Whistling Thorn- Damion is always seen with a few thousands of these tiny annoying little pellets. I don't know how they work but they can grow to the size of large balls, filled with various poisons and toxins surrounded by razor sharp titanium spikes. Initially starting at the size of a 6mm BB, he can grab a hand full of the little pellets and still, by some mystery they expand and grow spikes, screaming through the air as they approach with the sound of artificial grenades.

Dambe & Musangwe- The Ancient fighting style taught to him by his people is called Dambe-Musangwe and the name of the gauntlets that he wears. His fighting style is heavily based on punching and using his fist. The Gauntlets gives him punching power of over 1000lbs of force by combining the impact of his punch with a hydraulic thrust like a jack hammer. Simply, they are a pair of artificial knuckles with a hydraulic kick.

Air Drones- Damion has a total of four oval Drones that are each attached with very highly advanced mechanical computers and very durable outer cores. These Drones are normally seen hovering near Damion while in full tribal gear or he wears two on each leg as he stores them for travel. They have tracking, homing, infra-red, night-vision, remote viewing. They are also equipped with mini lasers and a self-defensive electric anti touch sensor. For some reason, they have the same expansion and contracting ability as the **whistling thorn** ability. This is where their defensive capability comes into place and they can grow and be used as a shield and when combined, all four shields can even create a great defensive wall that has enormous durability properties. Finally equipped with hover and jet propulsion technologies, they can be used in desperation as a blunt attack battering ram that can slam with and unmeasurable amount of force because we have yet to see its limits, the last tested impact force amount was over 10 tons of force at impact.

Light Cube- The Most Mysterious of his gadget is his ability to bend and control light. To be more specific his ability to absorb, or block light for a short period the cube is believed to be of another world and not truly a creation of Damion, believed to be a part of the ancient crystal that was broken into many pieces' years ago, its powers are undefined. But it seems this piece grants the ability to create an instant black void that catches the opponent off guard and Damion stalks his prey from the comfort of absolute dark. His technologies give him the advantage. The ability has been tested up to a 20-mile radius is its effective range and the effects usually last as little 15 minutes before the crystal returns all distortions back to normal, the cube can also bend light to create invisibility for a short period. We have seen no offensive abilities demonstrated in this gadget is only used for distraction and confusion.

Public Name: The Stalker
Real Name: Marcus Williams
Birthdate: Dec 15th
Age:25
Height: 6'
Eyes: Green
Hair: Dark Blonde
Race: Human
Occupation: Jack of All trades/ Demolition Expert

What do Demolition Experts Do: **Demolition experts** are usually contractors or construction managers who are experienced in wrecking and demolition work. These individuals are sometimes also called explosive workers, ordnance handling experts, or simply blasters. Individuals in a management position may supervise others in the most efficient and safest ways to demolish old buildings, homes, and other structures.

Work Environment: Since demolition experts often place and detonate explosives, the work environment requires safety measures to avoid injuries, and special protective clothing is often used.

How to Become a demolition Expert: Education required None; courses or vocational training in construction management beneficial. License/certification required to remove hazardous materials. Varies; 5+ years of demolition experience required. Strong analytical, decision-making, verbal communication, time-management, and managerial skills.

Background: Marcus describes himself as a free spirit. He played many competitive sports in school including football, baseball, basketball, soccer, and track and field. Never finding a real career to pursue, as he grew, he never stayed at a job after he mastered the position or learned all there was to learn. He learns through experience and ultimately ended his career as a demolition expert contracting for different private and government organizations. He became a bouncer at a local club, found a wife and lived a subtle life. To Protect his family, he uses an old, discarded demolitions

Suit from one of his prior contracting jobs. The suit is capable of incredible enhancements and unfortunately the company that designed them destroyed them before their competitors could copy the technology. He has learned to design his own custom ammunition that he keeps stored in Multiple locations around the city and in many underground tunnels that he has explored over the years. Marcus is a clever man although not highly educated his strategic planning is nearly flawless, there isn't much that gets past his ability to adapt and overcome using timed and well-placed explosives.

Description of Powers: Marcus is a part of the Williams family, he should be able to use the Ancient POWER GLOVES, but he doesn't. He chooses to use his Suit instead. The suit is Incredibly durable and was rumored to be tested in NUCLEAR EXPLOSIONS. Used to create secret tunnels under the city with secret entrances the suit is suspiciously light weight, increasing the wearers strength, endurance, and enhancing natural human ability, but with the bonus of 4 hidden chambers that hold controlled explosives of different degree. Ranging from Minor concussive blast to enormous explosions. Under controlled conditions one kilograms of TNT can destroy (or even obliterate) a small vehicle, but upon release 100 Tons is almost equivalent to a small nuclear explosion. We believe this is his Maximum Explosive capabilities alone, but if needed He can remotely detonate his entire arsenal in every secret location for a combined explosive force of well over 100-500 megatons of explosive force. This would completely obliterate the city and everything for miles but with his protective suit he would be the only survivor.

Concussive Blast- Small miniature explosives used in hand-to-hand combat. He places these on his opponents and catches them by surprise, the blast is usually enough to render most people unconscious with no collateral damage. No stronger than the blast of a grenade.

TNT SHOT- increasing in power this bomb is about the power on 1 Kilogram of TNT. These bombs can be remote detonated, proximity or explode on contact but these are some of the normal size bombs he uses in most battles. Very little collateral damage.

Final Warning- With the force of over 1 ton of TNT this is one of the few bombs that are used in fights with large demons or a horde of demons many opponents are not able to continue after being hit with one of these bombs.

It's Over (MOAB)- One of Marcus masterpieces, the MOAB is an explosion of over 10 tons and is the legal LIMIT of what Marcus can release on one opponent in battle it is his final attack if needed. This bomb can only be used in times of desperation.

Big BANG(FOAB)- Ranging from 50 to over 100 tons of explosive TNT force, this is the dreaded release of Marcus's full potential payload if he empties everything he has. But this attack would destroy the city.

JET- Marcus was given a custom-made that is his primary source of transportation. This bike can navigate the hidden tunnels throughout the city to avoid traffic or other obstacles. It's made of a Magnesium alloy and it's durable, it carries reloadable ammunition for the suit and custom-made ammunition for the bike.

Public Name: Madam CAT
Real Name: Angela McWaters
Birthdate April 29
Age: 27
Height 5'11
Eyes: Feline
Black and Brown Fur
Race: Feline/Human Hybrid
Occupation: Wildlife Biologist

What Zoologists and Wildlife Biologists Do
Zoologists and wildlife biologists study animals and other wildlife and how they interact with their ecosystems. They study the physical characteristics of animals, animal behaviors, and the impacts humans have on wildlife and natural habitats.

Work Environment
Zoologists and wildlife biologists work in offices, laboratories, or outdoors. Depending on their job, they may spend considerable time in the field gathering data and studying animals in their natural habitats.

How to Become a Zoologist or Wildlife Biologist
Zoologists and wildlife biologists need a bachelor's degree for entry-level positions; a master's degree is often needed for higher-level investigative or scientific work. A Ph.D. is necessary to lead independent research and for most university research positions.

Background: Angela was always considered a very smart and strong individual. She excelled at almost every class that she would take. Her only problem was that she was never social with people and always felt a strong connection to animals instead. She grew to become a Wildlife biologist studying animal behavior all around the globe. She was contracted by the Green Pond City government to investigate the effects that the green Water had on the local wildlife. Most of the animal avoided the water and the ones that consumed the water quickly died. One day while out doing her research she stumbled upon a rare natural species of cat, A mixed breed that rarely accrues between these two species. As she tracked the Cat, she uncovered an illegal group of animal trappers that had captured the cat and was about to execute the cat for his rare skin and coat. Angela screamed out and tried to save the cat. Angela was captured and tied up with the large cat and thrown into the green pond for disposal. While drowning, the green water merged with the Souls of the two, Angela and the Cat, extending their life and giving them a chance to escape. They safely returned to Angela's house, and she began to immediately get to work on studying what happened. She discovered that somehow the water had merged with their life energies. Angela gained the abilities of a feline, she was able to morph any part of her body to that of a CAT, her sense was heightened, and her natural abilities were enhanced. Meanwhile the CAT in which she named SAM, ultimately gained human like intelligence and the ability to stand and walk on 2 legs for a short time. Both of their souls have been merged therefore their life is combined into one, meaning that if one dies the other will die, that is why they are never very far apart. If you see Madam Cat, you can believe that SAM isn't too far behind.

<u>Description of Powers:</u> Angela is more extraordinary than we believe she even understands. Angela and SAM can jump as much as 20 times their height. The cat's peripheral vision is roughly 285 degrees, and they both can see in nearly pitch black with very little to no light at all. The ability to hear much higher-pitched sounds. The cat's sense of smell is 14 times keener than ours. they don't have to touch an object for the cat to sense nearby movement — changes in airflow can be enough. His tail helps him balance himself when climbing or jumping. The Tail is also used as a Whip and has many other uses as its maximum extension is over 100 feet long. Flexibility and Reflexes and not to mention her razor-sharp claws, and if that wasn't enough Sam is enormous and his power, speed and intelligence he will protect Angela at all costs.

Tail Whip: a 100 feet tail used to bash, grab, detain and many other uses. This is Angela's ACTUAL TAIL and is powered by her very muscles. It hits with about 3000 pounds of force per square inch. The tail expands and contracts upon will and there aren't any BONES in it that we are aware of.

SAMSON: Sam's history is a bit of a mystery for a cat. Currently he is learning more about his species' part in evolution. Sam is a genius, being a cat with human intelligence he has made better use of his mind than many humans. His Paw Strike hit with force of over two tons he has all his natural cat abilities but magnified.

Public Name: The Great Phantom
Real Name: Josh Williams
Birthdate July 7th
Age: 19
Height :5'6
Eyes: Gray
Hair: Brown
Race: Human
Occupation: Student

Background: The youngest of the two brothers, Josh Always looked up to Greg but he was never as skilled as his older brother. Josh studied dark arts, Blackmagic, Sorcery and witchcraft. While his brother studied analytics and biochemistry. Josh and his brother trained together with their father. He studied taekwondo and his brother traditional KARATE. Josh lost his family in the same tragic night as Greg by an unknown Assassin. Josh was arriving late from School when he met his brother. Together they opened the sacred box gaining the ancient Williams family POWER GLOVES. Each Glove amplifies the wearer's natural abilities but also adds a level of power based on the personality of the wearer. In the case of Josh, it became Umbra kinesis. The ability to manipulate light and shadow, stealing light and channeling darkness in the user's immediate surroundings. Josh can Manipulate Shadows in Numerous ways, because of his inexperience he is normally taking direction from the older hero's although his power is probably only rivaled by his older brother.

Description of Powers: Josh takes his knowledge of the dark arts and creates his unique ability to manipulate the Shadows. He can bend light to create, Solidify and command and army of Shadow puppets at will. His Shadow manipulation is granted by the Power gloves that he wears. These are ancient and enchanted gloves rumored to be passed down the bloodline by the GODS for the protection of EARTH and his family are the chosen protectors. With each of the four pairs of Gloves each member or close descendant of the blood line can activate a dormant gene in the blood that binds with the gloves and release the full potential of the individual wearer. Expanding the wearer's personality into a tangible power, the abilities of the gloves are limitless and the combinations of abilities they can produce are only limited by the wearer's personality and natural ability. Making them a weapon created specifically to be passed from each generation adapting each time to provide a defensive force for earth if the bloodline is preserved.

Living Shadow- Josh can turn any part or his entire Body into a living shadow effectively becoming immune to any physical damage. While in this state he also cannot harm anything physical unless the recipient believes the shadow can harm him.

Shadow Solidification- The power to condense shadows into a tangible form. Normally used for making weapons but he can use this in combination to Shadow Summoning as well.

Shadow Portals- Josh can create shadow portal through time space and worm holes. Connecting one Shadow Point to the Next he can Disappear and reappear anywhere he can see a shadow. With the limited ability to manipulate and bend light these portals can appear anywhere making josh very elusive.

Shadow Summoning- The ability to create Shadow Soldiers or Shadow Animals or any living creature. Once Combined with Shadow Solidification the Living creatures become servants of the new master usually fighting and dying for Josh.

The SHADOW MAN- One of Josh's most destructive Moves. Josh summons all of shadows and darkness within a 25km radius and locks it into place forming a huge giant shadow man. Then Combining it with shadow solidification the shadow man becomes a destructive force that is very difficult to take down because it's a giant living shadow.

-----------------------NOTHING FOLLOWS-----------------------

Public Name: Nuclear Man
Real Name: John Wagner
Birthdate: August 10
Age: 39
Height 5'10
Eyes: Brown
Hair: Brown
Race: Human
Occupation: Police Officer

What Do Police and Detectives Do?
Police officers protect lives and property. Detectives and criminal investigators, who are sometimes called *agents* or *special agents*, gather facts and collect evidence of possible crimes.

Work Environment
Police and detective work can be physically demanding, stressful, and dangerous. Police officers have one of the highest rates of injuries and illnesses of all occupations. Working around the clock in shifts is common.

How to Become a Police Officer or Detective
Education requirements range from a high school diploma to a college degree. Most police and detectives must graduate from their agency's training academy before completing a period of on-the-job training. Candidates must be U.S. citizens, usually at least 21 years old, and able to meet rigorous physical and personal qualifications.

Pay
The median annual wage for police and detectives was $61,600 in May 2016.

Capt. John Wagner and his partner Capt. Mark Jones Sr. were about to become Special Agents for the Government. On their last mission they were called on an armed robbery mission to help the local swat team as agent trainees. Reports say that upon infiltration, Capt. Wagner was confronted with one of the Armed men that attempted to run away. Capt. Wagner gave chase and inadvertently fell into a hole deep inside of a canyon under one of the buildings. Inside of that sink hole he claimed to have found this special, Stone This was an Ancient Stone buried away because its powers were known to drive a man insane. John became obsessed with the stone and soon discovered that he started to develop special abilities while in the presence of the stone. The Stone Gave him abilities. But in return John slowly loses his mind to the MADNESS of the Stone. Capt. Wagner's Profile says he has an iron will and doesn't break to temptation, but this is the ancient Chaos Stone, it's temptation of power grants madness as payment. Can John Control his anger to keep his sanity?

<u>Description of Powers</u>: Nuclear man powers are the biproduct of his relationship with the "Chaos Stone." The more he uses his powers the more he risks losing his mind to insanity. Managing his rage is important not to overdo it. Everything around you are made up of tiny objects called atoms. John can release nuclear energy through fission and fusion. Nuclear power is the use of nuclear reactions that release nuclear energy to generate heat. The nucleus of an atom is held together with great force, the "strongest force in nature." When bombarded with a neutron, it can be split apart, a process called fission. In nuclear fission, atoms are split to form smaller atoms, releasing energy whereas in nuclear fusion atoms are combined or fused to form a larger atom. This is how the sun produces energy. By harnessing the thermal energy released by the buildup of anger and rage, nuclear man can use inhuman abilities as his body essentially becomes a living nuclear reactor. He has the power of nuclear propulsion, nuclear explosions, nuclear heat waves, nuclear repulsion and even nuclear attraction, the ability for the nucleus to pull electrons towards itself. Also, Nuclear Wave the ability to release waves of powerful heat energy but short ranged, if too much energy is used at once He can become weak or exhausted. He can augment or diminish the fire abilities of others; he is able to send fire through any form of matter creating ruptures and create a pulse fire that can go through anything and depending on what Johns wants it can either be harmful or harmless. We are still running tests on the number of abilities that he can perform. I fear we have yet to see the full release of his abilities. If properly managed nuclear man's power could be limitless. When fully powered John begins to Glow very brightly.

<u>Nuclear propulsion-</u> Once enough nuclear power is gathered nuclear man can travel at great running speeds. We have Clocked him running at subsonic speeds of up to 500mph.

<u>Explosive Nuclear Orbs-</u> John can surround his fist with nuclear energy orbs and upon impact explode and send his opponent flying with a miniature localized nuclear explosive punch. Combined with nuclear propulsion this can become a very effective technique although close ranged.

<u>Nuclear Wave-</u> A very powerful concentrated but short ranged release of intense nuclear heat energy. This ability drains johns' power very quickly and nearly exhausts him completely, so he doesn't us it often as he would need to rest which could leave him in danger.

<u>Repulsion, Attraction, and Charging-</u> within close ranges, John can manipulate the atoms of inorganic materials and pull them towards him, push them away from him or manipulate its atomic structure to make it a nuclear weapon.

<u>Nuclear Meltdown-</u> If nuclear man becomes too angry and enraged, he could have a nuclear meltdown when he loses sanity for a brief period and his normal abilities amplify over 10 times in magnitude but what we fear is that during his meltdown, he could potentially become an endless series of atomic and nuclear explosions that can travel faster than the speed of sound and has unlimited nuclear power. It would be nearly impossible to take him down.

Public Name: Axel Blaze
Real Name: Axel Summers
Birthdate: February 9
Age: 24
Height 5'10
Weight:180
Eyes: Brown
Hair: Brown
Race: Human
Occupation: News Reporter

What Reporters, Correspondents, and Broadcast News Analysts Do

Reporters, correspondents, and broadcast news analysts inform the public about news and events happening internationally, nationally, and locally. They report the news for newspapers, magazines, websites, television, and radio.

Work Environment

Most reporters and correspondents work for newspapers, websites, or periodical publishers or in television or radio broadcasting. Broadcast news analysts mainly work in television and radio.

How to Become a Reporter, Correspondent, or Broadcast News Analyst

Employers generally prefer workers who have a bachelor's degree in journalism or communications along with an internship or work experience from a college radio or television station or a newspaper.

Background

Axel Summers and Greg Williams were best friends in school. Although Axel never followed the same studies as Greg. Axel grew to become a reporter and he loved being in the heat of the action if it was something happening LIVE. He became known for his dangerous coverage of live events, especially the top government heroes. He saw them as celebrities and to make a living. What most people don't know is that he is also a secret hero himself, chosen as a sort of deputy to Awesome Man. He is the Guardian of the Power gloves that rightfully belong to the Stalker, Marcus Williams. Only trusted by his best friend to protect the family powers, he normally only shows up during catastrophic events where he believes he needs to intervene. He doesn't want to play on the main stage as a government hero, so he is unofficial. He doesn't have any combat experience ordinarily, and he is considered and non-combatant hero. He's like a superhero first responder. He could cause harm, but normally he uses his powers to heal and if he is ever called into combat, he serves as a support and healing unit more than a combat unit. Be warned not to underestimate him, if he needs to do combat, he is well capable of dishing out enough punishment to make even the strongest opponent think twice about facing him. As a support unit his skills can be put to better use and as expected he reports on the action to his internet channel and has become one of the most famous reporters, but one of the rarest and least known heroes to be seen.

<u>Description of Powers-</u> Axel Blaze has the enormous powers contained within the Power Gloves. Normally these gloves only Bond to one bloodline per lifetime as they are the chosen guardians, but for some reason the gloves allow themselves to be used by someone outside the family, maybe because the bond between the two is so close. Axel Uses his powers to also defend the public but because he isn't combat trained, he normally uses his powers for support more. Power gloves can create matter based on the energy and spirit of the wearer and it's only limited to the wearer's imagination. Axel normally uses what he refers to as his Soothing Blaze to encase his friends in a healing and protective flame that minimizes damage and increases healing of minor injuries. But he has many more support items in his arsenal as well as offensive abilities he uses in desperate times. The abilities of his gloves are limitless, but he is the only owner that has ever used them in a supportive role.

<u>Soothing Flames-</u> The User can heal themselves and others by using healing fire, While the overall qualities of warmth and heat have long been associated with comfort and relaxation, heat therapy goes a step further and can provide both pain relief and healing benefits Heat therapy can help relieve pain from the muscle spasm and related tightness. Heat therapy dilates the blood vessels of the muscles. This process increases the flow of oxygen and nutrients to the muscles, helping to heal the damaged tissue. Heat stimulates the sensory receptors in the skin, which means that applying heat will decrease transmissions of pain signals to the brain and partially relieve the discomfort. There are several other significant benefits of heat therapy that make it so appealing. Soothing flames can also be used to Cauterize major injuries.

Electric Blaze- This technique can be used offensively, defensively or supportively. Offensively it can be used as a mid-level attack used to cause burn damage and ignite the opponent. Defensively it can be used to counter projectiles and physical attacks, and finally this technique can be used as an electric shock to revive or restart the person's heart if they stop breathing like a defibrillator. He uses it like electric extensions of his body.

Surgical fires of the divine goddess- Axel can summon the powers of the goddess and conjure the surgical flames of the gods. The gods lie inside of these flames to heal injuries their injuries. The flames are independently conscience, and they have their own will and can control their own destiny. These fires can heal a human that has been maimed or mutilated by using microscopic surgical fusions that manipulate the cellular structure of damaged and dead cells. It could bond damaged and destroyed tissue and cells including bone. If a limb is severed it can reattach and heal the limb to fully functional capabilities. Even severed heads can be re-attached, if this is not done fast enough the soul could leave the body and result in an undead being produced. Re-attaching heads or vital organs in order to bring someone back to life is risky but possible.

Public Name: Sound Wave
Real Name: Leyla Jones
Birthdate: November 12
Age: 18
Height 6'
Weight: 175
Eyes: hazel
Hair: Red
Race: Human
Occupation: Soldier

<u>Background</u> – Leyla is the daughter of Special Agent Mark Jones, trained by her father since birth to be a soldier, she was always a part of the Government recruiters' list of potential candidates. She grew up with her mother, and her mother and father were never married due to military service. Agent Jones would often visit his daughter between missions, and he would train her to be a great soldier. Once Leyla. Graduated Highschool he joined the military and was immediately transferred to the special agent's unit. She has average overall skill as a soldier and she was never as talented as her father, but she does have better technology skills than her father's generation. So, she develops a lot of the unique technology that her unit utilized. Since High school she had been working on a special prototype suit that can manipulate different types of sound and use them as a weapon. Originally, she designed the unit to be a Projectile weapon, but with military funding and great resources he was able to design a pair of gauntlets that can control various types of sound from a distance. she joins the Governments most elite Unit, the DREAM WORLD TEAM. Soundwave is a ranged combatant that disorientates and weakens his opponents from a distance. Her close combat is adequate but against a well-trained opponent her lack of experience shows, and she usually cannot sustain long term close combat battles with skilled opponents. She's better as a support to a team. Her gauntlets are impressive but on the grand scale of power that we have seen, it isn't enough to completely stop an opponent for long without assistance. Like all soldiers Leyla is skilled in various weapons and often her side arm and other guns are used as a more permanent way to stop an opponent after they are disorientated by her distracting and disturbing sounds.

Description of Powers- Sound can propagate through a medium such as air, water and solids. When sound is moving through a medium that does not have constant physical properties, it may be refracted (either dispersed or focused). The matter that supports the sound is called the medium. Sound cannot travel through a vacuum. The speed of sound depends on the medium the waves pass through. Leyla can manipulate sound and sound waves; she can release sound to attack. Using various shapes and intensities, either projected, used as a part of melee attacks. She can break the sound barrier, creating sonic booms that can cause severe internal and/or external damage to objects and beings. She can fly, glide and/or levitate through manipulation of sound.

Ultrasonic weapons (USW)
Sound Bullet- A short to medium range compressed sound and Air attack that hits the opponent with a Physical force.
Sound Explosives- Large Amounts of Compressed sound air and sometimes other elements that operates as a grenade, Land Mines or a Sound Cannon

Vibroacoustic Wave- Studies have found that exposure to high intensity ultrasound at frequencies from 700 kHz to 3.6 MHz can cause lung and intestinal damage. Extremely high-power sound waves can disrupt or destroy the eardrums of a target and cause severe pain or disorientation. This is usually enough to incapacitate a person. Less powerful sound waves can cause humans to experience nausea or discomfort. Leyla's Vibroacoustic Wave Drains a lot of the Suits Power and it can also harm friendly teammates, so she doesn't use it often.

Acoustic Levitation- Acoustic levitation takes advantage of the properties of sound to cause solids, liquids and heavy gases to float. The process can take place in normal or reduced gravity. Acoustic levitation uses sound traveling through a fluid -- usually a gas -- to balance the force of gravity. Leyla can use the ability of sound to levitate and hover. Flight is not possible however because although the sound pressure can lift Leyla in the air, it doesn't have the force to propel her in various directions with the ability to stop on demand.

<u>Sonic Boom-</u> Leyla's most powerful sound ability that has been observed is that she can create earthquakes at will, sound Induced vibrations causing an earthquake. With the release of all her power suit's ability into the ground Leyla can Level a City with an Earthquake.

Public Name: Issa
Real Name: Star
Birthdate: October 30
Age: Unknown
Height 5'6
Weight:180
Eyes: Red/ Yellow
Hair: Orange
Race: Alien (Brown Skinned)
Occupation: Astrology Professor

What Postsecondary Teachers Do
Postsecondary teachers instruct students in a wide variety of
academic and technical subjects beyond the high school level.
They may also conduct research and publish scholarly papers and
books.
Work Environment
Most postsecondary teachers work in public and private colleges
and universities, professional schools, and junior or community
colleges. Outside of class time, their schedules are generally
flexible, and they may spend that time in administrative duties,
advising students, and conducting research.
How to Become a Postsecondary Teacher
Educational requirements vary by subject and the type of
educational institution. Typically, postsecondary teachers must
have a Ph.D. However, a master's degree may be enough for some
postsecondary teachers at community colleges, and others may
need work experience in their field of expertise.
Pay
The median annual wage for postsecondary teachers was $76,000
in May 2017.

Background- Issa is a rare female alien from a very distant planet.
From her last known knowledge her planet is still alive and well.
They are an extremely advanced unified race. Being advanced
creatures, at birth each one devotes themselves to a lifetime
journey of discovery and exploration to obtain further knowledge.
Resilient to many of the hazards of space due to natural evolution,
Issa 's race has numerous beneficial abilities. She is the only of her

kind to come to earth simply to learn and enjoy the people and she will outlive us all. She plans to be here until earth's inevitable destruction which she has calculated but refuses to tell anyone because she is here to witness humanity evolve into star people or become extinct.

Description of Powers- Star is extremely resilient and her body tissues are extremely dense/solid, allowing them to withstand harmful forces on the body such as crushing weights, impacts, pressures, changes in temperature. Her knowledge of the solar system and time travel is immense and useful. Her various physical natural abilities are flight and solar blast.

Superhuman Durability- Star has survived the vacuum of space, entry and exiting multiple planet's atmospheres. Her body is not immune to pain or damage but her resilient and durability of her advanced body tissues mean she can take a lot of punishment before she begins to feel the pain. Regardless her healing time seems to be abnormally fast. Even fatal wounds seem to heal if given enough time. So far there are many things that can hurt her but not much we have seen that can Kill her.

Gravity Defiance- Star can walk on the air, treating it like a solid matter. She can ignore the laws of gravity, being able to levitate and fly, stand and walk on slanted areas or walls. Her movement is as if she treats the air like water. One of her natural abilities She moves around as if the laws of gravity do not apply to her.

Solar Manipulation- Star can create, shape and manipulate all aspects of a sun, starting from its immense heat, luminosity, mass/gravitational field, magnetic field. She uses solar energy in attacks of various shapes and/or intensities, either projected, used as a part of melee attacks, etc., from huge rays of pure energy that can knock over or even obliterate dozens of targets, or slightly singe them. She gains power from a source of solar energy/substances from a sun, concentrates it into a single point, and projects it in the form of a beam of destructive force that is capable of incinerating anything. Depending on the type of sun the user absorbs energy from, the beam's power can be varied. She has the power to create and launch balls of solar energy.

Solar wave- One of her most destructive attacks is the complete release of all her built-up energy. She can release massive waves of solar energy in every direction at once at almost unlimited scales. This power allows her to dispatch many foes at once and destroy large areas like cities and towns.

Lunar Manipulation- Star can create, shape and manipulate all aspects of a moon, including its gravity and the effects, reflective surface abilities and timekeeping. She can turn lunar energy into tools, objects, weapons and other items, create semi-living constructs and/or create structures/buildings of varying permanence. Users who have mastered this ability can use it for almost any situation, creating anything they need being limited to shaping from already existing sources.

Lunar Reflection- Star Can reflect whatever power is projected by her target and turn it back on them.

Public Name: Cyber
Real Name: Alex Cabe
Birthdate: None
Age: Unknown
Height 6'5
Weight:180
Eyes: Red
Hair: N/A
Race: Human/ Cyborg
Occupation: Military Soldier

Background: From birth Alex's body was created with
deformities and defects. He was not only born pre-mature, but his
physical body was deformed, and he would never have been able
to enjoy a normal life. Arms, legs, skull and spine were all
underdeveloped. Despite his physical limitations the doctors
detected that his intellect, awareness and cognitive abilities were
intact as normal. What they didn't know was that Alex had extra
ordinary intelligence, but his body was weak and fragile. Soon
after birth and various tests. Alex was cleared to go home, the
family struggled to financially support the medical expenses for
Alex. Things were not looking good until the family was
approached by a government agent, he offered the family a
proposal. The government would pay for all the medical expenses
for Alex, but the family had to agree to allow Alex to participate in
an experiment that may help. Due to the situation the family all
agreed, and Alex was taken away to be cured, but A combination
of Cutting-edge A.I software and Cybernetics were used to create a
unique and rare hybrid. Cyber the first human cyborg. Due to the
deal the government made with the family, Cyber would now be a
Futuristic Weapon. With his massive intelligence and a complete
arsenal of weapons at his disposal Cyber is a formattable opponent.
He lacks human emotion and compassion but his State-of-the-art
A.I Software can help cyber determine his decisions. Equipped
with a nearly indestructible metal alloy cyber grew to only know
combat and serves as a vital part of the government.

Description of Powers- Cybers' body host an enormous amount
of equipment ranging from Technology Manipulation to Guided

missiles and cannons. He can infiltrate cyber worlds and possess different machines and equipment if his body happens to fail on him. His Cybernetic conscience can inhabit almost any machine with a mother board. There are some ways that cyborgs can be equally stronger than ordinary robots. As such, they may have an actual brain rather than an artificial intelligence, thus making them think much more creatively or even perhaps have an AI, but with the AI and the person's brain working well in sync.

Artificial Limbs- Cyber possesses at least one appendage that has a wide variety of different functions and can be used for many different purposes. He can transform his arm into a bladed weapon, he also can transform parts of Himself (arms, legs, shoulders, etc.) into a strong gun-like weapon with massive firepower. no one can control the movements of such gun-like weapons when fired except a cyborg.

Cyber Manipulation- power to use the abilities of a robot/machine. He can use/imitate technological powers, he can become more like a robot, have the abilities of a television, be more like a computer and so on. he cannot transform into technology, as this power only enables the user to mimic machine traits while still in their original form. Some users can mimic multiple machines at once.

Nanite Control- The user can create, shape and manipulate nanites, machines or robots whose components are at or near the scale of a nanometer, more specifically, nanorobotics the tiny robots that the user's control can be programmed to build, destroy and cover themselves with metal. They can produce a suit of cyber armor made of sentient Nano-bytes that covers their body and is nearly indestructible yet still very agile. This power can upgrade vehicles or take over electrical objects using nanotechnology. The ability to wield or create nanotechnological weapons.

EMP Bomb- Cyber can produce a surge of electromagnetic energy, which can disrupt all technology nearby. The pulse may come from the user's hands or even from their entire body. An electromagnetic wave pulse that disables all nearby electronics, and no direct physical damage is induced. This is one of cybers strongest abilities. This attack forced cyber to Manually reboot his system once deployed so he becomes vulnerable. The Maximum radius is over 100 KM total electric, and technology shuts down.

Digital transformation- The ability to transform into or have a physical body made up of digital data. While in this form the user can travel through cyberspace, enabling them to access any device connected and enter its mainframe, some users even utilizing this to take overpower supercomputers from the inside.

Green Pond City's History: The Emergence of Power.
-Nearly all men can stand adversity, but if you want to test a man's

character, give him power.

-Abraham Lincoln

The sounds of the alarm are blaring, and everyone is rushing for the emergency exits. "Why are you just standing here Greg?" thinks Greg to himself. "It has only been a few months since you were assigned to this project and things have taken a turn for the worse. Since the discovery of that Green Water in the middle of the city the government tried to hide and cover it up, but the news came out. There is something in that water that naturally evolves the species to the next level of evolution but with the current DNA structure evolving so rapidly some people have been granted incredible abilities never imagined or available to the human body. But others, GOD what can I say, they seem like primitive birth defects, mutations, and more of a tragedy than a blessing to this world. I have been a chemist working with the government on trying to neutralize whatever is in the water. But the thing is, IT'S JUST WATER. I mean I worked with hundreds of the most intelligent minds and until today we have yet to find anything related to this water that distinguishes it from normal water. Well, besides the fact that it is green, and it naturally combines with hidden proteins in our body to unlock the keys to jump the evolutionary gap. This happens through consumption or external contact. The water has been named toxic; because of the uncertainty of the effect the water has. It seems to endlessly flow from an unknown source deep underground. Well, once the news came out about the water the crowds flooded to see this for themselves. Many people simply jumped into the lake; others drank the water. There were too many people willing to take their chance against the government with the dream of obtaining great power. The soldiers were caught off guard; they really underestimated the will of a people to get what they want. The rumors had been floating around since we discovered it and barely seven months later the city is in chaos, our government is losing to these creatures. I am supposed to be with my family today, but no time to worry about that now, I need to MOVE!! Once the mutants gained little control, they started attacking the scientist. Now we are being moved to a secure location, but I must get home. I must make it out of the lab on my own. If I follow the agents, I will be locked in hiding and kept from my family. The Government cannot cover it up anymore regardless of the theory they decide to go with. I have done my job; I cannot let them capture me; it is their fault for not listening. I need to get home to my family. This place will be crawling with those creatures soon." Greg changes into civilian clothes removing his lab coat, badge, and protective gear, pretends to be freighted and run to the firemen allowing them to escort him out of the building and to safety. He rushed to his vehicle and sped home, he could see people arming themselves with weapons and boarding their homes. Greg frantically tries to call home, but all cell service seems to be suspended. "I hope everyone is okay" Greg gets closer to his home and in the distance, he can see a fire blazing where his home is supposed to be. "No!" he cries out loud as he sees his house in flames. Greg pulls his car into the yard and jumps out so fast that his car has barely stopped. "CINDY!" "JOSH!" "MARCUS!" IS THERE ANYONE IN HERE?!" Greg screams loudly as he bursts inside the front door. The flames were everywhere but Greg pushed forward. "CINDY!" Greg screams out for his wife Cindy Young. Greg and Cindy are preparing for guests, his little brother Josh was supposed to be visiting from college and his older cousin Marcus coming for the holiday. Marcus said that he had important news and Cindy was making dinner. "If I had known there was going to be a mutant attack on the city, I never would have left her during the holidays."

Greg thinks to himself as he begins to cough. He is running out of fresh air. Suddenly there is an explosion in the kitchen. The gas line, the house is going to explode. "CINDY ARE YOU IN HERE!" Greg screams out as he begins to cough harder. "GREG, IM HERE!" Cindy cries out from the direction of the explosion. Greg rushes to the kitchen to see Cindy. She is pinned under some of the falling debris after the explosion in the kitchen. "GREG, HELP ME!" Cindy cried out as she saw her husband running through the flames to get to her. "MY LEGS ARE STUCK, I CAN'T MOVE" Cindy yells at Greg. "HANG ON, SWEETHEART I NEED TO FIND SOMETHING TO WEDGE AND GET YOU OUT.!" Greg yells back to his wife. "HURRY, THE GAS LINE IS BROKEN AND THE HOUSE IS GOING TO EXPLODE, GET ME OUT OF HERE!" Yells Cindy in a panic as she tried desperately to move her foot from between the debris. Greg Run into the next room look for something to help him free his wife. Suddenly, a series of explosions as the house begins to fall apart. "GREG!" Yells Cindy as the explosions continue. "CINDY!" Yells Greg as he attempts to rush to his wife, he enters the kitchen. Falling debris hits Greg in the head and the final explosion throws him backwards and out of the house onto the

yards. Greg passes out as his house falls apart with his wife inside.

DREAMS

"How was your day, Hun?" The Mrs. yells from the kitchen as she hears me plop on the recliner. She knows what I do for work and that I can never answer her with complete honesty.

"Fine Mrs. Williams, Thanks for asking" I reply as pleasantly as possible. To be honest, this entire marriage has been pleasant since the day I said I do. I have seen enough movies to know how it should go. I am supposed to be the "Best Husband in the World' I should go in there, pull her close by the waist and kiss her cheeks from behind, but I will settle for second best husband today, I really am tired from work.

"Marcus and Kristen are coming over for dinner tonight, said they had some big news!" said Cindy from the kitchen "Great, Company" ... I take the bad news silently and use it as an excuse to depart to the showers early.

Thinking back to the workday, I keep the shower short. We still do not know yet if the functions of the water applications intensify moods as well. I close my eyes; I need time to think about this more... I need to lay down for a second. Gregg retreats to the bedroom for about half an hour or so,

"How long was I out!?" I asked still feeling a bit tired…

"I let you sleep as long as I could dear." Cindy replied, "Hurry and get dressed, they'll be here any minute."

She stands in front of the vanity station I bought her for our 10-year anniversary. Still as beautiful as the day we met. sitting alone together in a small-town movie theater. It was interesting to see a girl in action and adventure movies. The rest is history. I strove to be her real-life superhero and she was the perfect 'catch'.

*Ding. Dong.

"They're here." We say in unison. I revert to the slacks, shirt, and tie she has laid out for me while she swipes pink lipstick on her lips and gives me a wink before she rushes downstairs.

"Coming!"

SECRETS OF THE FAMILY

"Sometimes life can be so hectic you know. I mean I don't understand what's going on here, has everyone lost their minds." Josh Williams, Greg's younger brother is shaken by the recent incident as he expresses his feelings to his cousin. "Be quiet Josh! He's waking up!!" Marcus Williams, Older first cousin to Greg and Josh notices that Greg is coming around after the explosion. "Greg! Are you ok?" asks Marcus "Yea, I think so." answers Greg. He is still a bit shaken as he wakes up. "Who is there? Where am I?" yells Greg Frantically as he remembers the explosion and the recent events. "Calm down Greg. It is me Marcus, Your cousin, and your younger brother Josh." "After the explosion we saw you were unconscious but breathing I brought you to this place for protection." Marcus explains. "From what?! What is happening Marcus, what do you know?" snaps Greg in an accusatory way to his cousin, suspicious that he could be involved someway with the death of his wife. "That is the same thing I asked him Greg, he keeps talking about someone trying to kill him and the family has secrets." Josh says interjecting the same accusatory attitude as his older brother. "Be quiet Josh!! I still have a headache and you are making things worse." Greg scolds his younger brother. The two have always had brotherly banter between one another, Greg always treats Josh like the baby. "BUT GREG We lost everyone in that explosion. We are lucky to be alive, there are mutants running crazy through the city, we have not seen each other in years and now in one day it seems the world and my life is ruined. We are hiding in one of Marcus secret warehouses from someone trying to kill us and you are worried about a headache!! I am not a kid anymore you and Marcus are going to learn to respect me." Josh yells at his two siblings who always seem to undermine him as an inexperienced kid since he is the youngest of the three. "BE QUIET JOSH!!!!" *They both yelled.* "Listen, I do not try to yell but this is hard for me too little brother, we have no time to grieve if we want to survive. I can explain the mutants, but I never expected my family to be targeted for assassination, we must listen to what Marcus has to say if we are to get out of this alive." Greg calmly explains to his little brother as he tries to de-escalate the situation. Greg has always been the calm and rational one of the three siblings, they look to him for leadership and decision making. He knows, now is not the time for a family feud and he needs to protect his younger brother more than ever now. *They both look at Marcus. "So, what's the story Marcus?" asked Josh.* "I am not 100% certain but I will tell you what I have experienced." Marcus begins to explain, "As you guys know I move around a lot. Well, last year I settled in this little town and worked as a bouncer in a night club, I met a nice young girl and me and her got serious and settled for a while in the nearby town. A few months ago, I received an invitation home for a family reunion today. Me and my new date begin making plans to come home and meet the family." Marcus explains as Josh interrupts "Ok, where are you going with this?" *Josh asked.* "Well soon after that invitation these accidents started to happen and a few times I was almost killed." Marcus continues to explain. "However, I got lucky, eventually after the third attempt I knew I was being targeted and I did not know why. Whoever it was murdered the girl I was dating, and I went into hiding I waited until I thought things had calmed down and I planned to come here and talk with the family about what was happening. I cannot think of any enemies I have that would want me specifically dead, so I guessed it maybe something to do with the family. No one followed me here and no one could have known

I was coming here except you guys, and Kristen, the girl I was dating." Marcus says as he concludes "I did not see the explosion, but I heard it. I got here as fast as I could, but Josh was already trying to wake you up. I saw him tell him to grab you and come with me here so we can figure this out and that is all I know. Josh what about you, do you know anything." asked Marcus as he concluded his explanation. "I was on my way here from school, midterms are over, and we were in due for a break. I received the invitation to come to the family reunion today too, but no one ever attempted to kill me." Josh says, "That is Odd", *Marcus stated.*

*"T*here was a strange feeling I had that someone was watching me, but I thought I was only stressing from schoolwork." Josh continues, "There seemed to be rumors going around campus about government secrets or something I do not know I do not care about those things, but it seemed serious and, on the flight here, security was tight for some reason it seemed they were looking for something, but if it is the government, they are always hiding something right?" Josh concludes still sounding lost and confused about what is going on. "Greg, what are these mutant freaks, you said you can explain them." Josh asks his older brother nervously.

"Well, the rumor is true Josh, the Government has been covering up the green pond in the middle of the city. Its natural water can evolve our species to another level we were still running test when people started to attack the facility and go after the water, the military was overtaken and we were all supposed to escape to a secret research facility to continue the studies, but I decided to come home and warn my family, that is when I noticed the explosion and now, I am here." Greg explains as his two siblings listen in surprise at the information. "It seems the military has started a counter offensive against the mutations already; they really were not prepared for this." Greg says. "So, what do we do now?" *Josh asked,* "it is dangerous out there, maybe we are being targeted. Not to mention the mutations, we cannot stay here we need to arm ourselves." Josh says franticly. "Well, I may have some things we can use" *stated Marcus.* "I have been trained in many areas of self-defense and explosives with a little chemistry thanks to Greg. I can create some weapons out of extraordinarily little material highly explosive stuff man." Marcus says excitedly. "Marcus, neither me nor Josh are qualified to handle that type of stuff we would blow ourselves up before we could be of any use."

Greg says in caution to his older cousin. "There has got to be something we can do, as much as I hate to suggest this, I think we should go back to the house and see if we can find out anything. Marcus, do what you can to keep us safe until we reach the house you are the most trained person here; I know josh has had a few Self-defense classes also, but I will put our safety in your hands." says Greg nervously. "The journey back may be dangerous, but I am confident we will be alright." Greg says. "There is something I must check on in grandfather's old basement him and the other elders of the family, even Grandmother would never let us down there. They were hiding something, and I believe it has something to do with why our family was targeted. Whoever it is will believe we are dead along with everyone else. I cannot force you two to join me but Marcus, Josh will you help me solve the mystery of this family can I count on you?" Asks Greg seriously and confidently to his fellow siblings. *They both excitedly agree and join Greg as all three cautiously exit the warehouse returning home to where their family died.*

THE MYSTERIOUS BOX

"Did you really have to wear that, Marcus?" asks Josh sarcastically "What my explosive protection suit?" Marcus answers. "Why not we have to be prepared for anything, I have a few demolition charges in the event we run across any of those mutants and this thing is explosive proof so I know it can take some damage in a fight and my abilities are enhanced in this thing." Explains Marcus "We received them as a part of the new emergency explosive defense squad, but the government shut it down because of funding and not enough contracts, we were supposed to dispose of these things in some acid-based chemical to destroy the evidence, but I just could not." Said Marcus. "Wait, wait, SO YOU STOLE IT!" exclaimed Josh. "Well, they obviously didn't want it anymore right; this bad boy is the last one left. Fully equipped with micro and Macro reloadable grenades and bombs usually used for demolition, controlled cave in and avalanches, and other useful explosions the government used to use. But technology has created more efficient ways to handle these types of things, so this is old tech. I have two clips of explosives left about 7 heavy bombs and 7 light bombs." Marcus explains. "Ok, so what makes the suit explosive proof Marcus?" asks Josh "I do not know all the science behind it All I know is it is made of these microfibers that Group together upon any impact over a certain pressure or speed and absorbs the energy from that impact. There are these sensors and paper-thin wires all through the cloth like material that make up the suit, once the energy from an explosion or high impact pressure is absorbed by these Nano fibers it is converted to energy for the suit to enhance natural abilities. Even the visors in the eyes have different visions to accommodate different situations. I wore this because considering our situation it seemed like a good idea." Marcus continues to explain. "Hey, you two quiet, were approaching the house we do not want any attention lets remain quiet if we can." Greg scolds his siblings encouraging them to stop all the chatter. "Ok Greg," *they both agreed. "*Where is everybody", *Josh asked* "this place seems deserted. Maybe everyone has been evacuated, there are signs of battle here hopefully the chaos has passed over this area. If so, we can search and find our answers in peace." Josh says. Suddenly, "HEY OVER HERE.!!" *Josh screamed.* Under the rubble was a mysterious blue box, As the three approached the box it started to glow very brightly. "What the hell is that thing?" *Marcus Asked.* "I am not sure" Greg said, "but it seems to react to our presence, and from the looks of it there are four symbols they look to be in the shape of a hand." Explains Greg as he tries to make sense of what he is looking at. 'Can we open it," Josh asked? "Maybe but it seems to be a bit of a puzzle there are no locks and no openings." Greg says confused. "I have seen this box before Greg, when you left, I was still a kid, but I remember mom and dad and our grandparents would always talk about some secret things in the basement and to never go down there. Do you think they could have been hiding something?" Asks Josh to his older brother. "It is possible, and it would explain a little of what is going on but what could be so special about our family." Greg answers. "But none of this adds up!!" Greg stated. He and Josh both grabbed the box, and their hands are suddenly covered with this black living cloth like material, "the hell is this, Greg!" Josh screamed. "Calm down Josh it does not seem to be harming us, I do not feel any different. As a matter of fact, I feel good." says Greg, trying to calm his little brother from panicking. "What is this stuff, and I cannot take it off?" yells Josh. "Can we take this back to your hide out Marcus and I can see if I can analyze it? Maybe find something to get it off and take this box back as well I would like to study it." says Greg as he tries to ignore his little brother jumping around attempting to take his gloves off. "That sounds great and all" Marcus stated, "but Guys I think we have a problem here." Marcus says nervously. Josh and Greg both turned around to see themselves being surrounded by the mutant creatures from Green Pond City. They had been discovered. "Greg, what do we do?" asked Josh. "We have no choice; we must defend ourselves!" Greg exclaimed. "It does not seem like they are going to let us leave. What do they want?" asked Marcus. "It does not look like a conversation!" Josh says sarcastically. "Marcus, I do not know what is in these gloves, but I feel confident That I am going to be OK." Said Greg to his older cousin. "How about you Josh?" asked Greg. "I feel strong, I feel aware and alert, I feel great." Josh replied. "Yea so do I." Greg says confidently. "Marcus, can you handle yourself?" Greg asked. "Are you serious, in this suit I was going to ask if you two were Ok I will be fine?" Marcus said surprised at Greg's question and sudden confidence. "Then let us see what these gloves can do." Greg says. "Josh remembers what Dad used to teach us growing up about fighting, remember the lessons. It is time to use them. Let us

Go!"

SECRET TECHNIQUES OF THE WILLIAMS FAMILY

-Simple techniques are usually faster and easier to apply.
-Master Yang Jwing-Ming

"I remember growing up as a kid," Josh starts to explain a memory

he has of training with his late father, Erik Williams. "Dad would

take us to his gym under the house. He wasn't home much due to

his job and travels but when he was home, he would always train

us in self-defense techniques and secrets he had learned on his

travels. I remember he always used to say, "there is no technique

which is perfect for all situations, what you do depends on what

your opponent does. opponents do not just stand there and let you

control them in battle; you must adapt to fit the circumstances.

using pressure point techniques, you must take your opponent by

surprise, pressure points control certain signals to the brain and if

you can catch an opponent by surprise and send a signal

unexpectedly to the brain you will shock the system and gain better

results. Once your opponent becomes aware of your intent, they

can mentally block the stimulation and regain control or their

body, in that case you must switch to a striking pressure point

technique to be effective. The best way to set up a surprise pressure point grab situation is to fake an attack to force the opponent to naturally defend or block then you attack the blocking limb as your true target. True Dim-Mak or death touch is used in the pressure point system so be careful, each strike or grab is used to injure an internal organ, and serious damage to the organs in extreme cases can cause death so know when to hold back. Grabs and pokes are used as light attacks or to create opening, strikes and bumps are used to stun or medium damage medium risk attacks, finally, if you can get your opponent stunned enough to safely attempt a finisher, crush your opponent with a devastating judo throw or switch to a limb twisting or breaking Chin-Na, to either set up for a larger combo and stun them further, or finish the fight completely. Remember, gain mastery over breath! breath is stamina and power reserves. You cannot simply choose a technique to use in a fight because a fight is dynamic, and its flow is usually always unpredictable. but if you are aware of a select number of techniques for various situations and are also aware of when to execute those techniques and some idea on how to apply them, you will be a much more effective fighter. I think this is what meaning behind the famous quote "be like water" many people fight and have a static set of moves that they will attempt to gain glory by performing. We do not ever want to fight and never want to cause intentional harm upon any other human unless it is in defense of my personal self or the greater good of the situation at hand. judgements must always be made, and we each can only hope that we made the correct ones when the time was needed. Ultimately all we have are our principles and what we stand for to make the judgements we are forced to make every day. When you intentionally attempt to strike someone, their body will naturally defend itself, even with no training, this is instinct. normally triggered by fight or flight instinct. The human body can change from soft to hard and the attacker could become injured in the process. All these things are governed by universal law that is set into motion by the actions you choose. Everyone faces the judgment of their actions. shame of self is one of the greatest punishments we place upon ourselves once we become more aware. So, to effectively apply a technique no matter which art you use, attacks should never be advertised or easily read by your opponent. The more you catch your opponent off guard, and keep them guessing, the more successful and a higher success rate of techniques can be performed. Even if poorly performed they can still be effective enough to gain an advantage or distance in a fight. This is helpful because if you are truly defending yourself, it could be enough to escape. I believe a fighter needs to learn the art of controlling the situation and more than less, the mind and the attention of his opponent. When you truly control the fight, you also control what your opponent does without them even knowing. Many fights are won in the mind before they can even be physically performed, defeat your opponent's mind, and the body will follow. also control yourself and control your breath, control your emotions, respect universal law, control your movements based on human limitation. Try to cleverly hide your movements so you are always attacking and defending all the time. There are only so many ways anything can attack you, learn defensive techniques for each of them. Control your distance and position in a fight because the law says it controls their equal and opposite position in a fight. techniques are performed based on location and position in a fight so the person that control location and position also gain limited control over which techniques that their opponent can perform based on their position and location and limitation of the body." Dad was a great fighter, but he always chose not to fight

whenever someone was upset with him. I only saw him fight

someone once, poor guy had no idea who he was stealing from.

someone managed to get into the house and locate his science lab,

they were trying to steal something he was working on for the

government, dad killed him. he thought I didn't see it because as

the guy tried to escape with whatever it was dad chased him, they

fought in the front yards and I look out the window, I should have

been in bed but within a matter of seconds after dad caught up to

him, I saw the man fall lifeless to the ground. As dad turned

around, I closed the curtain and lay in my bed. I never told him

what I saw.

SHOWDOWN

As the three men stand there with their backs touching in a tight
circle Greg begins to analyze the situation and prepare a battle
strategy…

"So, what's the plan Greg! exclaimed Marcus. I know you
are thinking of something, what should we do?

"I'm Thinking," says Greg. Now, I have no Idea what these
things are, but we are surrounded, and I can sense more creatures
on the way. Some of them appear to be human but some of them
appear to be animals and some of them I cannot tell what they are,
there is no definition. They do not appear to be intelligent…"

At that moment one of the creatures extended his arm from more
than 20 feet away. "HERE THEY COME," said Marcus. Josh was
caught off guard and the impact blasted him off his feet and threw
him back about twenty feet. His body hit the ground with a loud
thud, as he rolled to a Standstill. "JOSH!" screamed Greg. Before
he had a chance to worry about Josh, Greg had to protect himself...
"Father said to always keep your guard up, Josh was never good at
defense." Another creature attacks from behind, Greg is ready and

responds with a simple parry and strike. The force of the impact is strong enough to severe the creatures arm off. Greg delivers a finishing Hammer fist to the back of the neck sending creature crashing into the ground with a THUNDERING Impact Killing it instantly… "SO WHAT'S THE PLAN GREG, ARE WE KILLING THESE THINGS OR WHAT? exclaimed Marcus. "Yes, Said Greg, "Marcus, there are more on the way, use your bombs to keep the herd back and I will take care of the ones close to us, that way your bombs will not affect me, we must protect Josh and get out of here. "GREG LOOK OUT" screamed Marcus… The creature with the long arm reached out to grab Greg, as Greg tries to block, suddenly to everyone's surprise a transparent but bluish orb appears around Greg, crackling with sounds of lightning, the creature is deflected… "Now's my chance thinks Greg's, let's see what these gloves can do." He puts his hands together, as if to pray, "BACK OFF" screams Greg… Then He Pulls his Hands apart, at that Moment the Blue orb expands Electrocuting everything within a 50 feet radius All of the Creatures fall to the ground severely electrocuted to death. Marcus, stands in amazement unharmed because of his protective suit of course… "Marcus, your turn" ... Marcus still frozen in amazement…" Wow" Said Marcus, "You're Awesome Man, you hear me cousin, You Are Awesome, that was cool man." ... "Ok, but can you take care of the creatures please they are getting closer… MARCUS THE CREATURES!" Yelled Greg. "Ok, Ok Here we go let's try an artillery strike for precision, "The Rain of Hell" Yells Marcus as he unleashes a rain of tiny explosive bomb That completely irradicates the approaching herd. "Wow yourself, says Greg That suit is pretty amazing." ... "JOSH!" They Both Yelled. As they approached Josh, they realized he did not appear harmed. They reached out to wake him. "Josh are you ok buddy" asked Marcus. "Josh...?" Greg says… Slowly Josh lifts his head and opens his eyes. "What happened" asked Josh "Well, your brother here is Awesome. He can control electricity or something. He took all those monsters out with one move. He was all like BACK OFF! And …" "MARCUS!" "Enough, we worked together to protect Josh, are you OK Josh" "How are you alive after that?" "I'm not sure, I felt the impact and it felt inhuman took me off guard, knocked the wind out of me but otherwise I feel fine." says Josh … "OK So as I was saying, Greg was all like back off! Then, he electrocuted all of them. It was Awesome," laughed Marcus. "Is that true Greg" asked Josh. "Yea, apparently so, somehow, it's the gloves. But Marcus was able to withstand the intensity and he ever obliterated a herd of mutants by himself thanks to his, Codename Prototype STALKER Strike Suit 040506" laughed Greg… their victory was short lived as they were approached by a large mutant creature, this is when they realized how serious the situation really was. It seems as if the "Emergence of Power" from the Green Pond City has begun to affect and infest everything. What were they going to do, they cannot fight these things forever. They were never prepared to deal with something like this… "Josh, look at your gloves" said Greg "They are glowing". The large creature was casting a large shadow, Josh's gloves seemed to be affecting the shadow as well as the surrounding shadows. Josh stood up. "Hey, let's see what you can do," exclaimed Marcus. "Be careful," said Greg. Josh stretched out his hand and closed his fist, the shadows began to form into a large pile. Marcus and Greg Stood in amazement. "SHADOW MAN" Yelled Josh, and a large shadow-like Creature began to take shape and form, without josh giving any further commands, the shadow man protects Josh and begin fighting the large mutant creature. "As great as that is Josh we really need to get out of here before more of those things come. We need a plan. Marcus says", "I have an Idea I think I can help" says Josh... He reaches out his hand and opens his palm when suddenly a shadow portal appears, and Josh encourages them to enter the portal. "I don't know where we are going but ok," said Marcus. "Anywhere is better than here" said Greg and they all entered the portal.

BATTLEGROUNDS!

A large shadow emerges from the ground in the alley between two buildings, the shadow opens, and three figures walk out from the shadows. "I think I'm finally getting the hang of these things Greg," said Josh. "It appears that they are adapting to my thoughts. The Gloves have a way of manifesting my feelings and my thoughts. It feels natural to use them". Greg Nods his head in agreement, "I feel the same way little brother, I'm still not sure how it appears that each one of the gloves can manipulate a specific element. But for now, we can make the best use of them to protect ourselves until we can gather more answers on what is going on around here." Greg explains. The three stop suddenly and look at their surroundings, mutants are everywhere, there are people in the streets screaming for help, some appear mortally wounded or worse. There are government agents firing at the mutants as many of them fall back and run for safety. The roads are littered with human and mutant bodies, there are destroyed vehicles of all kinds, the buildings are in ruins and there appears to be no help coming for them. Marcus Activates his Suit "What do we do Greg?" he asks with expectations to fight. "We need to get these people to safety" said Greg compassionately. "They have nothing to do with this, we must do what we can to protect them first." Josh prepared himself this time "What do you have in mind?" he asks. Greg responds confidently, "We split up" Marcus looked confused. Greg continued the plan, "Marcus, you go and assist the agents, they do not have enough fire power to push the larger creatures back, eventually they will be overrun, if that happens, we will lose more lives. You must help them keep the hordes back and force the creature to retreat, at least buy us as much time as possible." Confidently Marcus begins to leave the group and head towards the agents "I trust you Greg, be safe" Greg turns to Josh, "I need you with me this time baby brother, how big do you think you can make those portals?" Josh looked puzzled, "I'm not sure but I will get them as big as you need, what are you trying to do Greg?" Josh asked. "I need you to get these people out of here as far and as safe as you can find, if Marcus and the agents fail to hold the creatures back then these people are in danger, the more people we save the less creatures there will be. These things are a reaction to exposure to the water, if more people are exposed then that is more, we must deal with. We need to save the uninfected." Greg continued "I'm going to get these people to you Josh, when I do, I need you to get them out of here." Josh nods his head in agreement. "I'll be ready for you Greg, go get them out of there. Greg heads off to rescue a group of trapped people in a small, abandoned shop. They are surrounded by three mutants; Marcus is already launching a counter offensive against the approaching mutants with the help of the government agents in the field. Josh thinks to himself, "I've got to find a way to get us out of here, the others are depending on me" He begins concentrating extremely hard on one of the safest locations he knows, a portal begins to form from surrounding shadows. "I've got to make it bigger if I want everyone to make it. He begins to concentrate harder, creating an even bigger portal, with all this energy being displayed he catches the attention of some of the mutants, and they begin to approach him. The others were busy, he could not call for help, he would have to continue to create the portal while defending it until help arrives. "I will not fail this mission" he thinks as he prepares to defend himself. His determination and willpower increase his power levels and his gloves are radiating a deep purple color, His body is covered in shadows only his glowing eyes can be seen, darkness forms around him. One hand concentrate on the portal and maintains it while the other begins to create shadow creatures of all shapes and sizes. These are his shadow clones. The shadow clones' glow with purple energy as Josh becomes more confident in himself and his abilities, "Keep them back!" Josh orders and immediately one by one the shadow clones began grabbing onto and holding the mutants in place, freezing their movements. Some creatures fall into deep shadow craters while others are dragged into other dimensions by the shadow clones. Josh notices that none of the creatures physically attacks anything. "I guess the shadows do not have the ability to harm things, it doesn't matter, as longs as the creatures do not reach this portal, we will be fine." Josh Thinks to himself. C'mon guys I cannot hold them much longer.

Marcus approaches the steel gate that blocks the entrance to the main government buildings. The Strike teams that have were deployed have been scattered and are falling back to regroup, there is a large mutant coming to ram the gates. "We must hold them back!" Marcus yells as a rally call for the scattered agents. His previous experience as a squad leader in the bomb squad is coming in handy. The agents get behind cover, but their attention is on Marcus now. Marcus heads towards the front of the gate running as fast as he can, "I've only got a few explosives remaining and then I need to return to my warehouse to restock on ammo." Marcus thinks to himself. Marcus is suddenly hit by a large flaming ball of gas, and the force knocks him off his feet. He rolls a few yards then stands to see what attacked him. A mutant stand before him with the ability to control fire. The mutant stands his ground ready to defend himself. "You are buying time aren't you" Marcus says to the mutant. Surprisingly, the mutant responds and speaks. "The human race is finished, the time for evolution is upon us, we must all drink from the waters of salvation and be purged of our sins." The creature continued, "Human, it is not I who is buying time but you, still holding on to your humanity when you can become so much more. We are all evolving, the result of evolution used to be something that one could only dream of ever knowing. But now, the government cannot keep this secret any longer. The Green water can transform a human into his ultimate evolved form, his true form". Marcus looked at the gate. The Giant creature was beginning to ram the gate and allow a horde of mutants to storm the government grounds as they attempted to steal the Green Pond Water. "So that's what they are up to" Marcus thinks to himself. The fire mutant prepares for his attack. "I WILL SHOW YOU THE POWER OF EVOLUTION!" The mutant begins to shoot flaming balls of gas at Marcus, "I've got to get closer" Thinks Marcus, I don't have enough ammo to have a long-distance battle with this guy, I've got to get close enough to make my explosives count." A flaming ball hits Marcus and knocks him down again, he rolls back to his feet. 'I can take his attacks all day in this suit, this suit can absorb much more damage than this, but the force of his blast is keeping me from getting closer to him or getting to the gate. I need to create a diversion" Marcus prepares himself for the counterattack, "I'll use an explosion of my own to counterbalance the force of his blast, this should get me closer to him faster." The mutant shoots another blast at Marcus, but he is prepared for it this time. "Concussive blast!" yelled Marcus as he fired a small rocket at the ground next to him. The force of the blast propelled Marcus through the air extremely fast, plowing through the flaming blast of air and crashing directly into the mutant. They both hit the ground rolling nearly 20 yards before coming to a stop. "YOU USED YOURSELF AS A PROJECTILE, AND THREW YOURSELF AT ME?" The mutant yelled confused and angry. "I'M GOING TO TEAR YOU APART WITH MY HANDS AND THROW YOUR LIFELESS CORPSE INTO THE GREEN POND MYSELF, I WANT TO SEE YOU RISE AS A NEWBORN." The mutant charges Marcus preparing to attack, Marcus braces himself, but the impact is so hard that Marcus is temporarily stunned. The mutant picks Marcus off the ground and then slams him back down to the earth with a thundering boom. The mutant delays his attack to admire his victory, "Did you expect another outcome? you are human after all and there is only so far that your body can go, even in that protective suit you are wearing." Marcus pulls himself together, the gate is breaking here comes the reinforcement if I do not do something soon. These things are stronger than I thought. Marcus loads two grenades in each hand as he stands to his feet. "I'm not finished yet, is that all you've got?" The mutant swings wildly with his right hand attacking with a traditional haymaker punch, Marcus slips under the attack and counters with an uppercut to the body. The attack itself does not even slow the mutant down, but before the mutant can counter, he notices the explosive attached to his stomach where he was punched. ““What's this?” ... “KABLOOM!!” The creature is sent tumbling backwards from the blast for more than 50 yards, a portion of his body was blown away in the blast. Marcus heads towards the gate but the mutant is not quite defeated yet, He stands to his feet as blood leaks from his stomach. The mutant sees Marcus running towards the gate and he prepares for his final attack. He begins gathering an enormous amount of energy into a large fireball. As he prepares to shoot the fireball at Marcus, he notices a flashing light on the side of his leg. Marcus had planted a second timed explosive on the creature during his counterattack in case the first one did not take the mutant down. “THIS CANNOT BE!” Said the creature as the explosive is ignited and blows his legs off sending his torso flying lifelessly through the air. “Such a waste of time” said Marcus to himself as he launches his remaining payload at the front gates. “Mother of all Bombs!” The giant creature and the horde have just broken through the gate and Marcus is out of time, the gate is breached, and the creatures are coming. This is all that Marcus can do. He stands watching as the explosives travel towards the mutants. "I hope this works; Greg was counting on me to keep these things back." The explosives hit their mark, it appears that it was just enough as the large creature falls in defeat and many of the horde scatters and retreats. There are still some that made it inside unharmed, but the remaining agents can hold them back for now. Marcus leaves to check on Greg.

Greg sprints towards the people trapped inside of the demolished building, there are three creatures that surround the building. Confidently Greg charges in, "With the power of these gloves I should be fine," thinks Greg to himself. One of the mutants notice Greg approaching, it is an animal-like creature that looks like a dog. The creature shows signs of aggression and begins to charge towards Greg. "Come on you bastard" said Greg to himself as he tried to activate his electrical powers. To his surprise, nothing was happening. The creature was getting closer… "C'mon, C'mon, C'mon, C'mon, C'MON" Greg says repeatedly as the dog-like creature jumps and collides with Greg. The dog has Greg pinned against the side of the wall of the building. Greg uses all his strength to hold the dog's snapping head back, inches from his face. "What's wrong with you c'mon WORK!" Greg says

demanding that his Gloves obey. His hand suddenly begins to

spark as the electricity started flowing through the creature's body.

It yelled in pain before falling to the ground. "who's next" Greg

begins to think before suddenly one of the other creatures swung

his arm in a backwards motion and hit Greg with enormous force.

Greg was sent flying about 100 feet in the air. He began to panic as

he tumbled helplessly through the air with anticipation of his

landing, "this could be fatal from this height" Greg thinks.

"Ground is coming up fast" Greg Braces for impact but realizes

that he is no longer falling. He looks and notices that he is

hovering in the air. "I can Fly!" Greg said excitedly "Now, let's

see if YOU can take it." He begins flying fast towards the ground

where the creature was standing. His gloves are glowing blue with

electric energy. "I hope this works" thinks Greg as he crashes into

the mutant with enormous electrical force. "TAKE THIS" he yells.

The force of the fall combined with the electrical charge is more

than enough to take down the mutant and leave a small crater in

the earth from the impact… Greg turns to come face to face with

the third and final mutant guarding the humans inside. This mutant is tall with multiple arms. "You must be the leader" Greg says as electricity begins to build around his hands. "There is no leader", said the mutant "We are simply a more evolved species, and this is natural selection. The humankind is weak we are here to show you the way." Greg Braces himself for an attack. The mutant grabs a fallen tree and throws it at Greg, who immediately dodges it. The Mutant runs towards Greg and takes a massive swing, Greg ducks under the punch knowing better than to block it seeing the Strength of this creature he hovers backwards to get out of range of his attacks. Greg Attempts to counter with a flying lunge punch, this was a high-level fighting technique taught to him by his father. The creature grabs Greg out of the air and slams him to the ground. Greg immediately rolls back to his feet "I will show you the results of my training" Greg yells at the creature as he unleashes a high-level combination attack, ridge hand to the temple, followed by a step-in back fist leading to a straight punch to the body, Greg finishes with a traditional left hook to the body and finally a knife hand strike to the opposite temple. Activating the meridians in both temples of the head and three well places attacks to the body, any normal opponent would have collapsed in defeat. As it were, the strikes did not even slow the mutant down, he grabbed Greg with 2 of his 6 arms and delivered two devastating hammer fist attacks on Greg before throwing his body to the ground and finishing with a stomp to Greg's abdomen. Dazed and confused Greg tries to regain himself. "My attacks are not effective, I need to hit him harder," Greg thinks, then he notices a large metal pole on the ground, Greg rolls and grabs the weapon, He stands and attempts to hit the creature in the head with the weapon. "HOW ABOUT THIS" Greg yells and swings with all his might, the mutant blocks the strike and knocks the weapon away, Greg immediately follows up with a powerful kick to the mutant's legs at the knee joint. The mutant stumbles backwards to catch his balance and in the process pushes Greg away. Greg Stumbles slightly but catches his balance, preparing to take advantage of his previous attack Greg charges his gloves and lunges forward with an electrical punch to the head, the mutants stagger again and begins to flail his arms wildly out of anger of being hurt. One of his arms hits Greg and knocks him down again. "I've got him hurt I've got to finish him" Greg thinks as again he springs to his feet gloves charged. Greg rushes in and delivers two electric charged hooks to the body, the Mutant starts bleeding, and in his rage, he grabs Greg again, blood pouring from his mouth. "YOU ARE AN ANNOYING LITTLE BUG!" He pushes Greg against a nearby wall, he attempts to Kill Greg by attacking with all 6 arms. Once he releases his hold Greg slips away between his legs. The attack demolishes the wall into rubble. Furious, the mutant turns around to see Greg Standing, beaten and bruised but still ready to fight. Greg Charges his gloves. "This will be my final attack" he says calmly to the mutant. The mutant is completely enraged and bleeding "WHY WON'T YOU JUST DIE?!" Yelled the mutants as he prepared to attack again but his legs were not moving, he seemed to be stuck, he looked down and realized that he was sinking in a black shadow puddle. "what's this?" The mutant says in surprise. "That would be my little brother." Josh had noticed that Greg was having a hard time with the mutant and sent his shadow creatures to locate and help Greg. The shadow creatures josh sent immediately attack the mutant immobilizing his movements, leaving a perfect opening for Greg. He rushes towards the mutant's gloves blazing with electricity, he jumps and connects a flying electrical punch to the mutant's head. The mutant slumps over and falls in defeat. Greg watches as Joshes shadow creatures drag his lifeless body into the void. He takes a

minute to catch his breath and rest before opening the doors to

release the trapped government citizens. "Come with me", Greg

says to the people as he leads them back to Josh. As he approaches

Greg notices that Josh is struggling to keep the portal open, there

are many mutant beasts trapped in shadows. "Oh GOD Josh!"

Greg thinks as he runs towards the portal, "C'MON HURRY UP, I

CANNOT HOLD THIS THING OPENED MUCH LONGER"

Josh yells as the crowd of citizens arrive with Greg. "Please get in

you will be safe I promise." Josh says welcoming their entry into

the black void. They all looked very hesitant at first but compared

to what they had been through and the sights around them they all

agreed to take their chance and trust these men. One of them asks

before entering the void. "What do we call you, who do we say it

was that saved us?" asked the citizen. Greg wanted to keep his

government affiliation a secret, he did not want to be blamed for

what was going on here today. Greg responded, "I'm just an

AWESOME MAN," Greg says jokingly as he mocks his cousin

Marcus from earlier. The citizen turns to Josh, … "and you, you're

like a PHANTOM or something with the shadows" … Josh thinks

to himself and smiles, "The Phantom, I guess it could be worse." He turns to the citizen and responds, "Yes that's fine, just please go NOW!" Josh demanded. The citizen turns and enters the portal, as he does, he yells thank you to AWESOME-MAN and THE GREAT PHANTOM… Josh turns to Greg, "Where is Marcus?" Greg Looks around "I don't know I thought he'd be back by now; he must have stopped the mutants because I don't see any reinforcements coming." Josh strains to hold the portal open. "Greg, I cannot hold this thing open any longer, it feels like holding a very heavy weight, not to mention keeping the mutants immobilized because I'm in no condition to fight." Greg silently agrees, "C'mon Marcus, where are you?" Greg thinks to himself. Suddenly, something can be seen in the distance coming towards Josh and Greg. "Do you see that, Greg?" said Josh. "Yea and I'm not sure what that is" Greg responds. He tries to charge his gloves but after his battle with the mutants Greg is exhausted. "What do we do Greg?" Josh asks. Greg remains silent focusing on the approaching figure, his heart is racing. If this is another powerful mutant, then that means Marcus was defeated. Greg fears the worst as the figure approaches. "Should we just get inside of the portal

Greg, Marcus will be fine" Josh says nervously. "WE ARE NOT LEAVING HIM" Greg says. He draws in his Strength and tries to charge his gloves once again. The figure is finally getting close enough to see a silhouette, it looks human … "ITS MARCUS!" Greg yells in excitement and relief. "DAMN IT COME ON! MARCUS I CANNOT HOLD THIS THING OPEN ANY LONGER" Josh yells as he really struggles to keep the portal open and hold the mutants in place with his shadows. Marcus is fast approaching, he can be heard yelling in the distant "I'm coming, I'm coming, wait for me." As Marcus approaches the others Josh reaches his limits, pushing himself so far, he falls unconscious to the ground. "JOSH" Greg yells surprised. "What happened to him?" Marcus asks as he approaches and nearly out of breath from running. "He's exhausted, we all are" Greg says as he notices the mutants have been released from their trap and are fast approaching. The portal closes, they are trapped…

A Peoples relationship to their heritage is the same as a Child to its mother.

-Dr. John Henrik Clarke

HISTORY OF THE KINGDOM OF AMARU

"Our true history spans 300 years, we, the Amaru kingdom, became a major regional power when we conquered the coastal kingdoms. With control over these key areas the Kingdom was able to establish itself economically and we had control of the state under divided ruling authority of the great generals who only answered to the KING. The king was the only absolute power for many years until my father's generation. His father had two sons, My father, and his brother my uncle. Originally because he was the oldest my uncle was named king for 3 years after the death of his father, the King, but my father thought that he was weak to be king. My father was the elite military general in the Amaru army, and he often challenged his brother for the crown. We were attacked one day from an invading army and many of our people were killed before the king reacted to the attack. My father bravely fought an entire battalion of the foreigners by himself and turned the battle for our people. But during battle the king had been killed. My uncle was slain and although he had a child, the child was too young to bear the title king. So, my father gained the title from inheritance from his father. My father was a warrior king, and he fought against the foreigners for many years before our people grew tired of war, and they started to believe in the customs of the New World. As our people became more involved with their people and their ways it started to change the behavior of the locals and many other villages. As my father grew older and his rule came to an end the people adopted a new system of choosing a ruler, I was voted out of my right to be the next king after my father. There are no more kings now, we call ourselves the family leaders. We gather and vote on different things involving our people and the community in general. No one has absolute rules anymore and our armies are all but a memory. The people have become a peaceful tribe many like me have re-located to the new world for a chance to rebuild and renew old customs, but this new world is nothing like our old land. The people here have not developed their spirit and are more aggressive. They are driven by a survival instinct; this causes them to only care for themselves in anything they do, and they have no sense of connection or unity. Their concepts and ideas are just as foreign as they are. They are a strange species non the less. My people have been victims of propaganda and have begun a life of struggle and misery in pursuit of a hoax. The foreigners are excellent story tellers, and they can put on a great display of talents, but they use their stories to manipulate the very belief system of another people, then they proceed to rewire the thinking system and reprogram the subject to behave according to its own will. My people have completely forgotten who we really are, many of them believe that their history started here on the new land. They have been completely brainwashed, and I let it happen. I did nothing. The history of my tribe the Amaru from our mother land Arunika, will not fade here in this land under a mind control spell of some sort. I am the rightful successor to my father, and I have made a mistake by allowing my people to come here or even accepting the idea that there was something wrong with our customs and cultures, Our beliefs, and our behaviors. The Amaru are a simple people, and it seems that my father was right all along. This government, we call it new, is not trying to help the Amaru people. It is trying to exterminate us. They cannot defeat us in direct combat because our technology is far superior to theirs, but they are highly intelligent still. They have infiltrated the common people and slowly through the years have become a cancer in my people. That cancer has now taken the last family I have, the history and existence of my people rest in my hands at this point. The last of my kind, I am The Last

King of Amaru, Eden of the motherland.

IT WAS A BLACK NIGHT, HEROES EMERGED!

`The Screams have stopped but I still hear the family crying as I approach. I can see the body lying on the ground from the distance, another one of our people was killed by "The Gang". I pay my respects to the family, and I need to speak to the family leaders. Tonight, I think the Black Nights need to make a reappearance. Since the migration to the new land and the dismantlement of the Great Kings our people have created their own secret government in an underground facility near the borders of the where the five great continents meet. Each of its leaders must be kept classified simply for protection. The fear of retaliation from the sun people has every nation feeling a bit uneasy. If I had my way, every nation that had a hand in the genocide and the destruction of my people would face the wrath of the Black Nights, but my family is no longer royalty, and I am only one of the family leaders who controls the last remaining secret dynasties of the Amaru. As I enter the room everyone can see the look on my face and my fellow leaders are prepared for what I am about to say. "Damien, we know that you are here to speak to us about the recent murders, but the Council still stands on our decision to keep the Black

Nights a secret until there is a real emergency." Said one of the older leaders. Another of the council members continued, "We understand your frustration but, think of how the five continents would react if they knew that the sun people still had the forbidden technologies of the Amaru." Still another Council member followed "Since the great migration of the sun you have been waiting for a chance to declare war. You are just like your father!" I Can no longer take this. "Look at the condition our people are in since the great migration! Look at how they treat us!" Damien continues "The GOVERNMENTS have not done anything for us since we have been here except to take advantage of our people with unjust laws and harsh punishments. Our people are brilliant, but we live in the worse conditions, and we do not receive proper support. Our people are being slaughtered by THE GANG and the government does not lift a finger to put an end to them. We have lost our history, we have lost our heritage, our families. We are a broken nation that secretly meets to talk about an enemy that you will not let me eliminate!" The council stands silent, Suddenly the youngest council member speaks. "Damien, I know that this is painful, and you must realize that the great migration affected every city in the Land of Arunika, not just your home of Amaru"

He continued "Each council member here is the last remaining

royal bloodline from Arunika, and even though many of us were

enemies in the past, for the collected benefit of our last remaining

people we must be cautious in how we decide to act in any given

situation." The Young council member had everyone's attention

now and the room remained quiet in anticipation of what he was

about to say. "Damien, you, and the remaining Amaru Black Night

warriors are our only military protection, and they cannot be

deployed because of a simple murder on government land. Our

people have no laws to enforce so our actions would be purely

vigilant. I know the Amaru were known for their technology but an

attack against the five great lands of this world would be suicide

for the remaining sun people effectively destroying any memories

of the great land of Arunika, our homeland. THIS IS BIGGER

THAN Amaru, this is about the restoration of the Arunika people

and a great migration back home." The room held their breath in

anticipation of Damien's response. "Much Resect young council

leader; your wisdom is beyond your experience, and you would

have been a great king in Arunika. I beg your mercy and ask that you just allow only one Black Night to be dispatched as a secret spy for my people, give them a champion, give them hope. If the Night is discovered, we have no government to connect to. He suffers and dies alone. But if he succeeds, we can finally know what the five nations and the governments are planning to do about the genocide of the Arunika people… or, are they planning to finish us off once and for all. Young king, we owe it to our people to give them the best chance of survival and the sacrifice of one Black Night is a fair price for peace and protection of his people. They are all trained to put their life on the line for Arunika and especially the Amaru." The young council member looks at the council and then turns back to Damien. "Whoever this brave Black Night shall be we must never know about it. You must understand that We cannot give permission for such things otherwise it become espionage. We agree that the people of Arunika need a Guardian and a protector but as a functioning government, no matter how secret, we cannot grant permission to disrupt any other government or people OFFICIALLY. Unofficially, whatever the Amaru does on its own time is of no concern to this council unless it jeopardizes the Arunika people. Damien you are the leader of the

Amaru people, the technology is from your family Dynasty, ultimately you are responsible for it." Damien looked puzzled, "what are you saying young council leader?" asked Damien. The young council member spoke carefully "I'm saying the Black Nights are yours and they always have been. We appreciate the protection of the Black Nights, but this council holds no authority over them, you are the commander of the Black nights, are you coming today to report that a Black Night member has gone vigilante?" The young council member gave a slight smile of approval which was followed by smiles from the other council members, but no one officially said anything. Damien stood silent for a second as he thought about all that had been said and he looked at the faces of the leaders, each with secret approval. He thought of his people. He answered "regretfully yes, there is a vigilant Black Night who has broken ranks and went to pursue the Murderer. I will keep the council informed on the activity of this Night until we are able to bring him home." The Young Council member smiled, "very well Damien and thank you for informing us of this, it's unfortunate. But it is not as unfortunate as the young lady who was also kidnapped along with the murder of her father.

All we know about THE GANG is that they are looking for the remaining leaders of the SUN people from the land of Arunika. If this brave Black Night has chosen, the path of a vigilante I only can pray that he does something worthy of honor and respect for his people and his culture. The council would like to be the first informed of the activities of this Night, and Damien the council will grant you classified information gathered among the Sun People so that maybe we can track the movements of this vigilant Night. We believe that he makes an appearance when his people are in need, and we would be the ones to know if the activity is worth investigation." Damien shook his head in agreement "understood, my fellow council members today begin a new Era for the land of Arunika and the broken people of the sun. Our redemption is near, I know the GODS favor your decision." Damien turns and walks out of the council room with his first mission, rescue the kidnapped wife of the murdered victim then report to the council. The Black Night will make its first appearance tonight. The murderers were heading in the direction of the Land of Moselle to hide among the citizens of Green Pond City and the pale skinned water people. I must be careful not to risk exposure of my people, therefore I will leave at dark. I need to

prepare.

'TWAS THE NIGHT BEFORE...

Damien leaves the council room; his mind is focused on his mission. "I'd better keep this a secret from everyone in the village." He thinks to himself. "If I were to ever be discovered anyone involved would be in danger." Damien runs hastily towards a small village to the east, "as the commander of the Black Nights, I may run into problems gaining access to the Amaru weapons and gadgets without official approval from the council, so I need some help, I need to see Malik" Damien investigates the sky and notices the sun going down. "I'm losing day light" The Amaru weapons are heavily guarded, if anyone including the commander seeks to remove any weapons from the weapons room then they need an order signed by the council. Amaru weapons are extremely rare and many of them are on a GODLY Level. The sciences and the technology involved with the Amaru people are highly advanced in comparison to their neighboring lands. This was the main reason behind many of the historical wars between the Amaru and other nations. Even neighboring countries within Arunika would often attack the Amaru to obtain the sciences and technologies that were being developed and used. The Black Nights never lost any war and eventually their only defeat was to a democratic people. Damien continued his journey, a man of peak strength and endurance he races to reach a distant village on edge the Arunika continent. "Malik is the only one I know with the equipment I need for this mission." His heart fills with pride as he approaches a giant tree. "This is the only way inside" Damien says to himself as he begins to climb the great tree. "Malik is an outcast from the Amaru and one of my most loyal friends I know he's here." Damien reaches the top of the great tree and overlooks a hidden village in the mountain. "Malik, where are you?" Damien thinks to himself as he begins to enter the village. "This place has no name and is never mentioned. There are no laws here, even the council has no authority here. If I get into trouble, it would be unbelievably bad. I do not have any support here, that's exactly why I know you are here Malik." Damien walks vigilantly through the streets of this unknown village, and he tries to sense his friend Malik. No one really pays him any attention but because of his training he cautiously makes his way to the center of town. "Malik where the hell are you?" Damien scans the town to see where he should go next, suddenly he spots it. "Malik you wouldn't" (GAMBLING

AND WOMEN) a sign hangs from a large building. Something draws Damien to this place. "Malik always had a problem with "Gambling and Women when he was in the village, as a matter of fact they are the very reason he was exiled." Damien thinks to himself as he enters the building. "Malik It can't be this easy" Music plays very faintly in the distance and Damien looks around but to his surprise no one is around. He continues and goes deeper into the building. "Malik, I know you are here" Damien thinks to himself. Music begins to play from speakers inside of the surrounding walls, Damien prepares himself for the worst as he positions his body in a defensive fighting stance. "What business does the prince of Amaru have in this village" a voice says over the loudspeakers." Damien scans the room for threats. "There must be a surprise attack coming soon. Probably some sort of projectile to incapacitate me." Damien thinks to himself. "C'mon if you are going to attack" Damien yells to threaten the voice as he prepares for the obvious trap. Suddenly, three doors open and one after the other incredibly beautiful women begin walking out towards Damien in very revealing clothing. Nearly twenty women appear and begin surrounding Damien, but they do not say anything.

Damien continues to scan the room. Money starts to fall from the ceiling. "All of this is a distraction" Damien thinks to himself. "The falling money obscures my view" Damien pauses… "Here comes the real attack" Damien hears a faint humming noise approaching. The women begin to dance, as Damien prepares for the attack.

The music plays louder and louder, and the women dance faster and faster, Damien looks in all directions. "Pay attention to a change in the pattern, all of my senses are blocked, whoever this guy is, he's smart." The women on the right began gradually moving to one side, creating an opening. Damien notices, "THERE!" He thinks to himself, as a flying drone shaped projectile comes blazing towards him. Damien easily ducks under the flying projectile, then he noticed the women on his left began to move to one side. "Another one?" The drones shaped projectile comes at Damien fast, in this position he has no choice but to jump over it, another miss. Damien lands, but before he could plant his feet to gain his balance, he notices the women to his front and behind him both step to one side. "Two attacks at once" Damien thinks to himself. Not able to gain enough balance to jump, Damien twists himself and pivots on his toes, leans his head to one side and bends his body backwards as the drone shaped projectiles both cross in front of him nearly inches from his face. Damien falls to the ground but quickly recovers, as he stands on his feet preparing for the next attack. He notices that the women have begun leaving the room and going back through the doors they came. The music lowered, and the money stopped falling from the ceiling, Damien lowered his guard slightly. "You are going to have to do better than that if you want to take me down" Damien yells out loud. "I don't think you know who I really am" Damien continues. "Oh, I know perfectly well who you are Damien". The voice over the speakers announced. "It looks like you have gotten stronger since last I've seen you" the voice continues. Damien pauses, the voice does not sound familiar, this could be another trap. "Who is this guy" Damien thinks to himself as he prepares for the next attack. "I've got to find a way out of his kill zone and locate the attacker, I cannot defend forever. Damien begins scanning the room for something that can transmit a radio signal. "Those things are being remotely controlled somehow and moving at those speeds there must be a transmitter nearby or the person controlling them must be close." Damien thinks as he looks around, but a transmitter could be hiding in anything. As Damien searches the room four doors open and each of the four drones emerges from the doors. Each surrounding Damien, they are hovering in place, and they do not seem to be attacking. Staying vigilant Damien thinks to himself, "Watch the change in pattern, start looking for a way out". The lights begin to go dark, and Damien can hear the doors around hit begin locking. "I'm trapped, DAMN IT, my only hope is to capture of those things and see if I can redirect it to smash my way through one of those doors." Damien thinks. "My timing must be perfect" As Damien prepares, he notices a figure standing in one of the doorways. "That's him" Damien thinks "and my way out" Damien changes from defensive to offense as he prepares to take this guy out. "You should have never shown yourself, now it's my turn!" Damien announces confidently as he begins to charge towards his opponents. The four flying drones begin to come towards Damien. "It appears as if they are armed again" Damien thinks. "Here they come" Each of the drones come flying at Damien with extreme force, and one by one

Damien dodges and defects them accordingly as he makes his way to the figure standing in the doorway. The figure is not running away but standing and watching Damien face off with the flying drones. "They seem to be operating on a magnetic power system, but their patterns are very predictable so it's easy to dodge them." Damien thinks. "They strike with such force so if one hits me, I'll probably be knocked unconscious. I must stop the one controlling them." Damien gets closer to his opponent. Carefully dodged his way there. "If this guy isn't running, he must be very skilled in close combat" Damien thinks as he gets closer. "I must not underestimate him, if I had my Black Night armor and equipment this fight would have been over." Finally, an opening! Damien is close enough to launch his first attack on the figure in the door. Damien rushes fast and gathers his strength. "WHO ARE YOU" he screams as he throws an immensely powerful punch.

SECRETS

As Damien lunges forward towards his opponent launching an immensely powerful punch, the four drones magnetize and connect with each other forming a large shield. The shield flies fast toward the figure standing in the door and he catches it just in time to counter and block Damien's punch, but Damien has a trick up his sleeves also. "How about this" he yells. Damien is wearing a pair of specialized gloves he designed to complement his fighting style of Dambe. Once the glove connect with a direct hit Damien can trigger a Hydraulic thrust to his punches increasing the force by nearly two Tons of force per square inch. Landing a direct strike with such force that many cannot even withstand the weight of the attack even if it is blocked. The mysterious man holds the shield firmly but unexpectedly Damien releases his super punch, and it catches his opponent off guard. Even though the shield blocks the punch, the weight and pressure of the attack is more than enough to blast his opponent backward towards the wall with such force that he is thrown through the wall. CRASHHH!!! Rubble and debris from the destroyed wall flies in all directions. The mystery man crashes through the wall and rolls for several feet before the inertia from the punch is dissipated. The four flying drones fall to the ground, lifeless and the mysterious figure struggles to stand to his feet. Damien walks slowly towards the hole in the wall to face his defeated opponent." It's time to get to the bottom of this and locate Malik, I have more important thing to attend to than this distraction." Damien thinks as he approaches his weakened enemy. "You really don't recognize me do you" the mystery man says as he coughs a little blood. The light begins to shine through the broken wall and finally Damien can get a good look at this opponent that caused him such a headache. "Who in the hell are you? Identify yourself or my next attack WILL kill you!" Damien Says in a demanding voice as he recharges the hydraulic glove. The figure stumbles towards the light, Damien sees a slight smile on his face, and recognizes him immediately. "MALIK" Damien yells as he rushes toward his injured friend. Damien grabs his friend as he begins to fall, holding him securely Damien asks, "What the hell are you doing Malik, why would you attack me?" Malik gathers his strength and stands to his feet. "Well, it's nice to see you too" Damien looks at Malik seriously without speaking.

"Ok, look I wasn't attacking you, I was testing my new equipment, the Air Drones" Malik Said. "I saw you come in my place of business, and I decided to give you a proper welcome for the commander of the Black Nights and one of my best friends." Damien looked puzzled. "Besides, like I said I wanted to test my invention, but I never expected you to react like this, what brings you out here anyway? "Malik asks Damien. "I needed to see you" Damien answers lowering his guard. Malik and Damien would always compete when he was in the village to see who was better, Damien should have expected his friend to try to surprise him. "I'm sorry Malik, but something important has come up and I need your help to do this." Malik continues to gather himself, "What in the hell did you hit me with?" Malik asks. Damien smiles "This is just something I've been working on, increasing the pressure and power of my punches to take down enemies faster using hydraulics." Damien answers his friend. "That felt like at least two tons of punching force and pressure in order to have that type of effect" Malik says. "It was" answered Damien. "That's incredible, well what can I help you with since you have shown up and kicked my ass, again" said Malik jokingly. Damien looks at Malik silently for a moment and then "I have secretly exiled myself from the Amaru Village and reactivated the Black Nights without permission of the council. I am going to infiltrate the Green Pond City and pursuit the Gang that continues to kill and terrorize our people so that I may gather enough information to find out what is really going on with the Government. If I can prove that the Government is allowing the destruction of the remaining people from Arunika it may be enough evidence to restore the Black Night Armies with the Council permission and then the Arunika people will have a fighting chance to restore our culture and resources of our land. I believe that integration was the trap that finally destroys our people and the only hope they have is for us to act now. We need to migrate back home rebuild and regrow our customs and culture otherwise we will fade away." Malik looks at Damien for a long time as he tries to take in everything that his friend has told him. "You are serious aren't you" Malik says. "Yes, my friend I am" Damien replies. "What do you need from me?" Malik asks. "Weapons, and equipment mostly but you also have to keep this a secret" Damien replies. "I've decided to live a dual life and not let the village know what I'm doing, I will be the only person investigating this mission." Damien says. Malik looks worried, "That's suicide Damien, one NIGHT is not enough to take on the entire government and the GANG, even for the commander of the Black Nights, are you crazy" Malik says. "That's why I need you my friend" Damien says. Malik looks puzzled, "I was exiled from the Amaru because of my crazy weapon inventions. The Amaru Army has much better equipment than I do. Why not get your weapons from the Village, I mean you are the commander of the Army, right?" says Malik. "I just told you, this is supposed to be secret, if I try to gain access to the equipment, I will gain suspicion and this mission is not approved by the council." Malik looks nervous but supportive. "Malik, I need you, there has been another murder, and someone has been kidnapped. No one is doing anything about it, and I am not going to allow any more deaths. Will you help me" Malik thinks to himself, "well I did want a chance to test my equipment to see how effective it is, and Damien is my friend" Malik looks at Damien with a serious look. "Ok, I'll help you, but remember most of my equipment is prototypes and I cannot guarantee how effective they will be, so you must use them at your own risk." Damien nods to acknowledge that he understands. "I knew this would be risky, and I appreciate anything you can do to help. But you are the only one I can trust, we grew up together, you are like my brother Malik." Damien says. Malik Smiles "OK My friend let's do this." Damien investigates the sky, it's nearly time to start the mission, darkness falls, and this is the best time for infiltration. Malik notices the look on his friend's face. "Look, I only have limited equipment now, it's not easy getting material and funding for the type of science needed to create Amaru grade weapons and equipment." Malik Says to Damien. "Do you have any Metal Organic Fibers (M.O. F's)" asked Damien. Malik pauses before he answers. "I do, I was only able to obtain and cultivate a little of it. It is hard to get." said Malik. "It will have to work for now, so where is the suit?" Damien asked anxiously to begin his mission. "See that's the thing, I didn't make a suit with the M.O.F. material" Malik said nervously, as he knows he is speaking to the prince of Amaru and the Commander of the Amaru army. The Amaru are the founders and the creators of the M.O F. most of it was stolen and used inappropriately. "Well Damien my friend, I have raised four cultures of M.O.F.'s but instead of molding them into power suits like the Amaru, I molded, my cultures into to the Air drones that you fought earlier" Malik looks at his friend and smiles "Before you say anything, they are one of my most successful and USEFUL inventions to date, if I do say so myself." Damien looks at Malik puzzled. "Wait, so those flying things are living metal" They operate in their own individual conscience?" Damien asked very curiously. Malik again looked a little embarrassed to tell his friend this but responded respectfully. "Yes, I raised them like any M.O.F. They are about 5 years old now, and they are beginning to develop different personalities. They still have not fully matured, so I am still learning a lot about them, we are still bonding." Damien was impressed and demanded to know how Malik uses the living metal fibers inside of inventions that failed to work for Amaru scientist. "I was raised to believe the M.O.F could not be easily cultured; how did you do it?" Damien asked, "and make it quick, I must go soon!"

CREATION OF POWER

In the early years of the Amaru, many of the great kings focused much of their wealth in the development of new sciences. Before the land of Arunika civilized itself into tribes and villages, many of the people there would pass away due to unexplained illnesses and disease. As the people grew higher in conscience and leaders began to arise, the very first thing that the Arunika people discovered was the microscopic world and the many ways to manipulate it. Wars begin to divide the people and the land. As people grew in conscience the population developed different variations of similar beliefs. To keep the peace, many of the great leaders decided to live in harmony with the surrounding lands and not fight over them. The last remaining families that survived the wars migrated to different parts of the land to grow their village and their family. One of the main families, the Amaru tribe began to focus most of their studies on science and combat. The Kings believed it was important to defend his people from everything small and large. During the rule of Jelani's Grandfather is when a breakthrough in the sciences happened. The King allowed the scientist to experiment with creating new forms of organic material. This is how the M.O. Fs were originally discovered. The scientist was attempting to create a special metal for the king. The metals were made by combining inorganics with organics using special bonds. Negatively charged inorganic ions of large metal oxides bond to small positively charged organic ions inside of an artificial cell to mimic the internal structure of a biological cell. Modifying the Metal Oxides fibers with characteristics of the membranes of natural cells, gives control over the chemical reaction of the metal. Many materials were tested until the scientists were successful with only a handful of compatible metals. Just like any organic life this metal needed time for the cells to divide and grow. It takes years for the metals to mature. Once mature, the metals can manipulate the size and nature of its structure without changing the topology. Also, the thermal and chemical stability of Metal Organic Fibers combines with varying arrangements of functionalities giving rise to materials that offer synergetic combinations of properties. The M.O.Fs are porous and breathable material that exhibits high surface areas with potential for numerous applications and uses. The only downside is that it takes years and special material to produce these metals. After the metal-based cells begin replicating themselves and evolving they can absorb an enormous amount of energy and use this energy as a food source, storing energy like a battery until the energy is needed. Also, because the cells are organic, after a certain amount of energy is absorbed and consumed, energy waste is released in the form of liquid bioelectricity. Liquid bioelectricity provided an enormous renewable energy source for the Amaru and was used in everything that powered the city. This technology was discovered while developing a new Armor for the KING that would help him in battle. A few of the prototype and test suits were STOLEN but ultimately the suits were perfected. The King loved the suits so much he ordered that every member of the Black Night Army be cultivated and issued a special suit for them. Years later the beginning of the Black Nights and their amazing stories of battle. The Amaru scientist never took the research any further because the mission was simply to create an Armor. The Black-Nights embraced this armor but never thought to create weapons from this metal. Weapons can be lost in battle and the enemy may retrieve and duplicate the metal. The king feared this and so the metal was supposed to be used for armor only. Once the king discovered what

I was creating with the metal I was immediately discharged from the Black Night Army and exiled from the village. The King ordered that no one used the metal any other way for protection of the village. Therefore, you have never heard of the metal being used for anything besides armor because it was your grandfather who created the law inside of the village. Once I left the village, I was able to experiment with the metals that were inside my suit. I did not want to destroy my suit, but I needed the rare metals that It was created from. Unable to effectively severe a piece of the suit for duplication, I learned to breed the metals. The suits are a rare exo-suit composed of M.O. F's and certain unknown metals. The metal is light weight but extremely durable and can take enormous punishment. The organic metals in the suit can shrink or grow to uniquely fit the wearer. Metal is self-healing, so if damage does occur to the metal, it can completely heal on its own given time. During times of major repair and healing the suit can reject its wearer and require days of healing before it can be worn again. My prototypes were mostly inorganic metals, so they did not have this problem, but it was not as versatile as the newer models worn by the Amaru today. My personal suit is the base of my experiments, mostly I keep the metals impregnated to continue to produce metal offspring, but each generation becomes less and less Organic and more unintelligent metal. Since my protective Black Night suit was being used to reproduce offspring, I am not able to wear it. So, for protection, after one of the first cultures of the M.O. Fs were birthed and reached maturity I began to develop and mold them into a protective shield. The shield began to divide itself until four unique metal shaped drones emerged. The metals stabilize and they are in their final form. From here they can only learn and adapt to their environment. They have been raised to protect their owner at all costs. They do not possess the unique healing factor of the Amaru Newer models, but their durability is increased more than 20 times as much as an Amaru Armor. The amount of damage these things can absorb before they need to heal is unbelievable. If they join and form the larger shield the damage absorption can be up to 50 times as much as the Amaru Armor before healing is needed. These things are fast, and they think, learn, and adapt to the enemy they are fighting. As you have seen they are so intelligent that the owner does not even have to give a specific command for them to automatically defend themselves from incoming threats and dangers. They can split up and do multiple

things simultaneously and one of my favorite features is that if you

ever need a ride, you can just use one as a personal hovercraft. The

only suit I have is one of the first models before the M.O.F.'s was

developed. I understand that you are in a hurry Damien, this is all

that I can offer you now if you want it. well, there is one other

thing the whistling thorns, my very first weapons. Quite simple but

particularly useful combining all this together, with your training

and those crazy gloves, you would be a deadly foe to anyone who

dares oppose you, even without the protective armor of the Amaru.

What do you say Damien? Would you like to take my equipment

for a test drive for me? I will design all the weapons and material

that you need for your journey, you just need to have an open mind

and bring me the material I will need to continue my experiments.

THE FIRST NIGHT

Damien investigates the sky, the sun has gone down, the night has begun. "Malik it's time, I must go now, I have a long journey ahead of me." Malik hands Damien two wrist bands. "Here wear these, this is how the drones know who to be loyal to." Malik says snapping the metal bands around each wrist "You must continue to train them; they obey verbal and visual commands" Malik continues. "Thank you again for all of your help my friend, I promise to return them safely" Damien interrupts his friend. "They are yours now Damien, consider them a gift" Malik says happily "Besides, you'd probably make better use of them than me, now hurry" Damien changes into the old Black-night uniform. Loads his hydraulic glove, stocks up three pouches full of whistling thorn, and summons the flying drones" the drones begin to hover around Damien moving synonymously with is movements. "They will begin learning everything about you including the way you move and fight, eventually you will not even have to give them any command, they will obey your very will as it will become their own." Malik advises. Damien smiles "That's good information my friend, I'll keep that in mind. Eventually, I am going to have to name them, it may be bad Karma not too. Besides, I do not want to keep calling them Drones" Damien says jokingly. Malik and Damien laugh "If we survive this mission, I'll name them but for now let's go DRONES" Damien commands as he jumps into the air and is immediately carried away by one of the flying drones as the others hover close to ensure his safety. "I'll see you soon my friend" Malik says to himself as Damien hovers out of sight. "This is great, you'd think I invented these things by how easy it is to fly them" Damien thinks to himself as he heads towards the border of Arunika to the Land of Moselle and towards Green Pond City. "I still do not feel comfortable without my armor, but I'll manage somehow." Damien thinks to himself. On foot this trip would have taken at least a 2-hour running nonstop to reach the borders, at 28 miles per hour." Black Nights are trained to run for at least 4 hours before complete exhaustion. The average Black Night can run at least 15 to 20 miles per hour and maintain those speeds for varying hours depending on the Black Night. Damien is the leader of the Black Nights and can maintain his running speeds for hours. But these things can fly at 100 times faster for 100 times longer. Damien approaches the border as quietly as possible knowing that the Moselle government must have some defenses. To his surprise no one was guarding the border between the two lands. "what's going on around here?" Damien questioned himself as he continued hovering towards the city with no opposition. He had crossed into another land, and no one had even noticed. "This is too easy" Damien thinks. The city is only a few more miles away. Cautiously he gets closer and closer towards Green Pond City. Damien used to work in this city with the rest of his people that immigrated to the new land in hopes of a different future after the kingdoms were dismantled. He worked as an engineer for most of his short career. Most of their technology was old and outdated so the jobs were quite simple. That was until I received the call from my sister about the Gang and what they were doing to my people. I came back home to protect the remaining Amaru people. Damien gets closer to the city and notices something is wrong. "This place looks like a warzone." Damien hovers higher "How am I supposed to find her in all of this" Damien thinks as he hovers above the city. "From high up all the destruction seems to be spreading outwards. "If this continues it will reach Arunika and I cannot allow that. Whatever this is I have got to stop it" As Damien looks around, he thinks about what his father told him "Always look for the change in the pattern" Suddenly he notices right outside of the city, looks like a small town, there are lights on there. "A peaceful town directly outside of a chaotic city", Damien thinks, "Let us go have a look" Damien bypasses the city and makes way towards this mysterious town. Approaching cautiously, he notices a light patrol outside of a secluded house. "The hell are they up too?" he asks himself. Damien jumps off the "Drones" and motions for them to remain quiet. Surprisingly, they obey. Damien quickly scales a tree and perches on a nearby branch. "There are four of them" Damien thinks to himself as he begins a battle strategy. Four armed mercenaries are patrolling an abandoned house. "There seems to be activity inside of the house, but I cannot see inside." Suddenly a women's voice screams out "SAIDIA, SAIDIA" from inside of the house. Damien recognizes the language and accent immediately. She is from Arunika. "This is the place" Damien says to himself as he completes his plan of attack. Damien Leaps from the tree to the roof of the house, there is one here, a spotter. Damien creeps slowly behind the mercenary, before he even noticed, Damien kicks out his knee from behind and catches him in a rear naked choke until he passes out. Immediately he jumps off the roof onto the back of the second mercenary catching him by surprise. He falls to the ground dazed and confused but before he can react Damien gives him a hard chop to the carotid artery and the mercenary is out cold. He turns to attack the other two Mercenaries simultaneously with whistling thorns, a well-placed aim into the heads. But before he could attack, he noticed that the flying drones had already taken out the other two mercenaries quietly just like Damien. "Great Job" Damien thinks, "if you keep this up, I may just keep you." The four drones converge on Damien as he prepares to enter the house. "Let's keep this quiet you guys, I'd prefer to remain undetected." He enters slowly, there is a large room to the rear of the house that has a light on, the rest of the house is dark with no power. Damien approaches the large room. He dispatches his drones to the four corners outside of the house. Preparing himself for the worse Damien enters the large room. He sees the wife of the slain Arunika Villager from earlier. She is tied to a table and being injected with a green substance from machines. "SAIDIA" the woman screams continuously. No one is around so Damien approaches the table to free her. Letting his guard down he did not notice a large figure watching from the corner in the next room. Desperate to save her Damien rushes in ignoring his training and triggers a trap. One of the floorboards is triggered with explosives. Damien attempts to counter the explosion by shielding himself with the fireproof Cloak, but he was not fast enough. The explosion launched Damien through one of the windows and out of the house. Damien is shaken but ok. He stumbles to his feet confused. "I was sloppy, should have known it was a trap" Damien says out loud to himself. A large figure approaches. "I agree with you, whoever you are, it was obviously a trap" Damien gathers himself quickly, He never even noticed there was someone else. The four drones surround Damien and prepare to defend him. Still shaken a bit, Damien says in a stern voice. "WHO THE HELL ARE YOU?" The figure gets closer, and Damien is shocked by his appearance. Damien takes a step back. "This guy looks dangerous" he says to himself, what is he going to do? The figure steps into the light with confidence. He says to Damien "Most people call me The Judgement of Doom, I'm usually the last person you'd like to see because if you see me then you are usually already dead!"

JUDGEMENT NIGHT!

The large figure emerges from the shadows so Damien can have a good look at him. Damien takes a large leap backwards while simultaneously grabbing a hand full of whistling thorns. "You can call me Judgement for short if you like" Damien keeps his guard up, cautiously keeping his distance from The Judgement of Doom. "Are you frightened by what you see?" The Judgement asks. Standing at over 7-foot-tall, wearing a helmet custom made of a large ape skull and elephant tusk, a tactical uniform with various explosives, guns, and throwing knives. On his back was strapped a large looking assault rifle. "So, you are some kind of assassin I presume" Damien says confidently. "Oh, I'm not just any assassin" The Judgement answers. Damien notices the assassin reaching for the gun on his back, it was very subtle, and many would not have seen it. "he's a quick shot, I've got to move" Thinks Damien, as he leaps into the air and throws a hand full of whistling thorn, immediately one of the Drones carries Damien back and away while the other 3 take defensive positions preparing for a counterattack. "And I am not that easily defeated!" Damien yells, the Whistling thorn scream through the air as they grow, and the razor-sharp thorns are aimed directly at the Judgement. These little things are Malik's first invention. Inspired by a scared tree Malik infused the living metal into pellet sized metal balls that expand and swell to about 10 inches around and nearly 25 lbs. each. Combined with razor sharp metal thorns, when these things fly, they whistle alerting the enemy but usually difficult to suddenly defend. They are great weapons for surprise attacks as well as direct assaults. When thrown they expand and swell quickly so they are more useful at short to mid-range for direct attack. Just like any thrown weapon, longer distances require more of an arch when thrown but with the sudden change in weight during swelling the whistling thorn, are not very reliable at longer distances, accuracy and trajectory are greatly reduced and unpredictable. Be that as it may, Damien counters this by using the Drones to increase his height and speed when throwing them and therefore he is able to counteract the additional weight and trajectory. Perfectly aimed, the Whistling thorn began falling towards earth directly over the head of Judgement. "This is going to be fun" The Judgment thinks as he immediately grabs the Rifle on his back. "Explosives!" yelled the Judgement, suddenly his rifle begins to change shapes into a large grenade launcher. He fires three grenades at the whistling thorn, the explosions are enough to change the trajectory of their fall. The whistling thorn fell to the earth completely missing their intended target. The Judgment stands as the smoke clears unshaken by the attack. "Cute trick, but I have tricks too" the Judgment says to Damien teasing his attempt to surprise attack him. "That I can see" Damien says noticing the metal on the rifle. "That Gun is made from M.O. F's?' Damien asks rhetorically. The Judgement is taken back to Damien's instant knowledge of the secrets of his weapon. "Very observant my friend, no one alive knows the secret of my weapon and you correctly diagnose it within a matter of second, who in the hell are you? The Judgment asks curiously. Damien, never slowing from his attack, circles around on his Air drones and leaps into the air towards the Judgement. "I am your worst nightmare" Damien says to intimidate, The Judgement fires a grenade, but Damien is easily able to dodge the grenade as he closes in for a close strike using the abilities of Dambe. Damien throws an attacking punch at the Judgement. Before the strike lands the judgement once again reaches for his rifle. "SHIELD!" yelled the Judgement. The rifle once again Morphs into a giant shield. Almost perfectly the Judgement blocks Damien's physical attack. "I was counting on that" said Damien and then he released the hydraulic kick. KERCHING! Although it was blocked, the inertia and force behind this attack threw the Judgement off balance and he tumbles backwards. Desperate to regain his balance, The Judgement grabs two large blades from each side of his tactical pants and slams them into the ground to slow himself. Standing at his feet, "you are just full of surprises, aren't you? I'll make sure to avoid that little gauntlet of yours next time." Damien did not hesitate with his assault, the attack had separated the assassin from his rifle, Damien noticed this and continued his offensive. "I'm not finished yet, let's go drones!" Damien yells as he leaps into the air and throws a hand full of the whistling thorn. Simultaneously landing on one of the hovering drones, he points his finger at the Judgement of Doom and without saying a word the remaining three flying drones begin to attack the Judgment. Hoping that the combination of attack will at least slow this guy down, Damien jumps off the flying drones at a distance and watches as the whistling thorn begin to grow and fall to the earth, the drones were keeping this guy busy. This must work Damien thinks confidently. The Judgement dodges the predictable movements of the drones, also lacking the fourth drones that Damien is using for protection and mobility the three drones themselves lack the formation and the timing needed to land a direct hit. "This guy is really good" thinks Damien as the whistling thorn gets closer. The Judgement investigates the sky and sees the incoming attack. "I've got to deflect them" the Judgment thinks. The first drone attacks again, the judgment dodges to the right and tosses a tiny sticky grenade on the drones. The other two drones attack simultaneously, the Judgement leans back nearly at 90 degrees and tosses two sticky explosives on the bottom of each. Keeping his momentum going he flips his body backwards and pulls out two grenades. He throws the grenades into the air as he stands to his feet simultaneously pressing the trigger in his hands. A massive explosion erupts and shakes the ground and the surrounding area. The whistling thorns are thrown off their trajectory and the flying drones begin to spiral out of control until they crash into the ground. The judgement stands in the smoke from the explosion. Damien cannot see his face, but he knows that he is probably laughing. "His technique is nearly as precise as my own training." Damien thinks. "The only option is to take him out in close combat, I am the general of the Amaru military I will not be defeated here." The two men stand at a distance for a while as they prepare for the battle, they know is to come between them. They have both eliminated each other's weapon and although they would never admit it to each other they have gained respect for each other. "This was supposed to be a simple mission" the Judgment thinks to himself, "Who the hell is this guy?". SAIDIA!! The woman screams from inside of the house. "There is a member of Arunika trapped inside and I need to save her" Damien thinks to himself, who in the hell is this guy?" The two begin to walk towards each other. Damien prepares himself for an attack. He keeps the remaining drones close as he waits for the others drones to repair themselves and return. Only a few whistling thorns are left but he does not want to waste them. The Judgment Stops and yells out. "Take her, I'm not getting paid enough on this job to face a Black-Night." Damien stands in surprise but relief. "You know of the Black-Nights?" Damien yells back as he notices the Judgement picking his rifle from the ground and placing it on his back. "of course, I know of the Black-Nights." I helped create them!" said the Judgment of Doom, as he turns and begins walking away. "Wait, what?!" yells Damien. SAIDIA yells the woman from the house. "Tend to you people NIGHT, we will meet again" said the Judgement as he disappears into the darkness. Damien immediately rushes inside to rescue the woman. "What the hell was that all about?" Damien questions himself as if he is finally able to complete his first mission.

A NIGHT OF HONOR

Black-night watches as the Judgment of Doom walk away into the darkness. Carefully the Black-night re-enters the house to free the citizens of Arunika. There are no traps, and it appears to be safe. Slowly, Black-Night disconnects the medical tubes connected to the hostage to stop the flow of this mysterious green chemical that was being pumped into her veins. "This is inhumane" Damien thinks to himself. "Come on, it's over now I'll get you to safety. Damien walks out of the house holding the weakened woman. By now the Drones had all recovered from the explosives." Let us go home you guys, it has been a long Night. Damien hops onto one of the flying drones, he places the woman on another, the drones begin to expand and reshape itself to cradle the injured passenger. Damien notices the intelligence of the Drones. "You guys are pretty smart, take care of her and get us home" Damien commands the Drones, without hesitation they obey and begin the journey back to Arunika. "I need to see the council" Damien thinks to himself. "This woman needs serious medical attention." As Damien hovers back to Arunika he begins to think about the battle with the Judgement of Doom. In his mind he tries to analyze his fighting style and remember his moves and tricks. "I'm sure we will face each other again, and this time I will be ready." Damien says to himself as he thinks about the mistakes he made during this fight. "I need to see Malik again, and you guys did good, I guess it's time to give you all names. Damien tries to relax as the Drones enter the land of Arunika and begin towards the location of the council. "Let's see," Damien says aloud. "He looks at the drone that is hovering and providing protection as they travel back home. "I will call you Waruhiu, the weapon. You are usually the one that is ready for a fight." Next, he looks at the drone that appears to be hovering at a distance and providing perimeter alerts, seeking to locate and identify enemies before they become a threat. "I will call you Adilah, the one who fights to be equal, not as aggressive as your brother Waruhiu, but eager to show your equality in combat support." Damien takes notice of the drone that chose to carry the hostage and put all its trust in the other drones to protect it. "I will call you Gasira, the one who is brave. Willing to fight and protect." Finally, Damien gives acknowledgement to the drone he seems to always use as a personal transportation device. This drone seems to always want to stay close to Damien and provide whatever support he needs, even if it is just a ride. "I will call you

Enam, because you are God's gift to me, my own personal servant

that chooses to never leave my side." The four prepare to descend

close to the location where the council usually meets. "Gasira,

Adilah, Waruhiu, and Enam Lets' Go!" Damien command. The

four drones obey without hesitation and begin their descent to the

hidden location of the chamber of the Arunika council. The

security alerts that something is approaching, and Damien expects

to be approached with hostility, everything he is doing is unofficial

and no one is to know who he really is. The council is summoned

immediately as Damien lands, he is surrounded by the Council

Guards. Immediately the drones take defensive positions, but

Damien is not worried. A member of the council approaches

Damien, and he gives them the injured victim. "She needs medical

attention, they were injecting some king of green chemical into

her, she is alive but barely, I suggest extracting a sample of the

chemical from her blood stream and constructing and antidote."

Damien says firmly to the Council member that approached him to

retrieve the victim, "who are you?" the council member asks. 'I am

a friend of Arunuka, I am the rouge Black Night" says Damien. He jumps onto Enam and soars off to see Malik again. The council

member gives the Arunika victim to the medical team and the

scientist. "This woman is to be cured and diagnosed immediately."

He orders. I just hope we are not too late…

A NUCLEAR CATASTROPHE

"The unleashed power of the atom has changed everything except our thinking. Thus, we are drifting toward catastrophe beyond conception. -Albert Einstein

I remember the night that the call came in…. "Are you ready partner," asked captain Mark Jones to his partner John Wagner. "Yea, it's about time", said Captain Wagner, "We are the best officers this city has produced in a long time, we are finally getting a mission to prove ourselves." Possible bomb with hostage. Swat and special forces are being called into action. Captain Jones and Captain Wagner are trainees of the special forces program and were not supposed to take any action unless instructed. "Once all the teams were placed in position, we received the order to sweep the building slowly. Communications have been disconnected and we could not verify if the hostages were safe, in addition, we must verify if there is even a bomb." said the team leader…. We enter the building, trained to maintain noise discipline, I look at my partner officer Jones, he gives me the look to be careful, but I am ready, I can feel it, this guy is still here. I have always been one step ahead of Mark. He is more cautious and calculating. He comes from a good family background, good parents and all. There are people at home that he must make proud. Me on the other hand, no one cared, and I like it that way. I am going to prove that we deserve to be a part of the special forces' unit. I am going to catch this guy. I worked hard for everything I had. I am the best at my job, and it is time that people finally recognized it. Mark goes right, I go left, we are listening for anything, and then suddenly… Movement. "MARK OVER HERE I Yelled", Something moved. We were in a large open area, there were only two ways out of this place, the way we came, and the door in the back. "THERE!" screamed Mark. "Do you see that" "Yea, I responded I Do, but what is it." Me and Officer Jones Both saw this creature and it was not human. It had the trigger to a bomb in its hand, once it noticed us, he tried to escape out the back door, but I refused to let it get away. I was closer, so I gave chase, I told Mark to back me up, but he said that orders were to call for back-up, we are not trained to handle a bomb." He stayed behind to report and call for back up, but I knew that if I stopped this thing, I could stop the bomb. It ran through the back door, and I was not too far behind it. What happened next is hard to remember. There was a Giant hole in the ground on the other side of the door. It caught me off guard and of course I fell. The creature, believe it or not, was flying away as I fell. But here is where things get weird, I do not remember ever landing anywhere just falling. "After that I heard a very deep and intimidating voice speak inside of my head that said, "EMBRACE ME FOR I AM YOUR SALVATION" there wasn't much I could do to fight it, so I just relaxed and let it happen, "And Now I'm here" Said Captain John Wagner "So What happened after that "Asked John. "Well, John I'm glad you asked, it seems there really was a bomb and once you opened that door in pursuit of this thing that you and Officer Jones saw, it exploded." We found you more than 50 yards away with two broken legs. There were never any hostages that we found." Said the Police Chief… John had found himself in the hospital with unknown injuries but by a miracle he survived an explosion. The chief of police and the Director of the Special forces Unit were there to see him. John would live, but he could no longer be on the force due to his injuries. Although devastated he was more concerned about his partner. "What happened to Mark" Asked John. "I'm Sorry," said the Director, but Mark was close enough to the explosion to receive injuries. He volunteered to allow the special forces unit to administer an experimental treatment in exchange for a position on the special force's elite unit. The treatment was successful, and he is now in recovery. Once he is rehabilitated, he will be in service with the

Government. I know that you two worked hard together, and I am sorry that you will not be joining him, but he needs your support now. John smiled "That's good news, I'm glad one of us made it in. No one better than Mark, he deserved it more than me, I'm proud of him." Said John. "Is there anything that I can do in the department." asked John. "I'm sorry, but I didn't give the orders," Said the director "Truth is John, your legs will heal, but there are some officers that think that you are a liability, a loose cannon. Top Brass sent orders to give you a medical retirement, a full ride, no more work. They didn't want you to know but I think you deserve to know the truth." Said the director, "Is that true Chief" asked John. I'm afraid so, my hands are tied, but look at it this way, you can just take it easy now, you've done enough for this city, just cheer for Mark from the sideline and don't cause too much trouble." As the truth of the situation began to emerge John began to get upset. "CALM DOWN FOR NOW JOHN" said a mysterious voice "I TOLD YOU I WAS YOUR SALVATION, I WILL GRANT YOU MY POWERS, BUT IN RETURN YOU MUST FEED ME ALL OF YOUR RAGE, ALL OF YOUR ANGER ALL OF YOUR PAIN AND HURT, SERVE ME AND I

WILL HELP YOU." "Who are you" Whispered John to himself so the others would not notice. "YOU WILL FIND OUT SOON ENOUGH, FOR NOW HEAL YOURSELF." Said the mysterious voice. John agreed to retire in peace but vowed that he would return to help his partner again one day.

SECRETS OF THE CHAOS STONE

Months passed and John had not taken retirement very well. His legs have healed but there is severe nerve damage, and he is only able to walk and not run. He drinks alcohol a lot and starts a fight wherever he goes. As John stumbles homes this night, disappointed in himself, nothing really to live for. He hears a familiar voice inside of his head. "JOHN, IT IS TIME FOR YOU TO AWAKEN YOUR TRUE POWER", says the voice. "Who are you and why can I hear you inside of my head." demanded John. "VERY WELL I WILL TELL YOU OF MY EXISTANCE AND I HOW CAME TO BE, WHAT DO YOU WANT TO KNOW?" Said the mysterious voice. "What is your name, who are you?" asked John. "I HAVE BEEN GIVEN MANY NAMES OVER TIME, BUT CURRNTLY I AM KNOWN AS ABRAXAS." Responded the voice. "How are you in my head" Asked John. "DURING THE EXPLOSION, THE CREATURE THAT YOU WERE CHASING WAS A DEMON, THE BOMB WAS NEVER MEANT TO KILL BUT TO RELEASE ME. THE STONE THAT I LIVED IN WAS DESTOYED ONLY A FRACTION OF THE STONE REMAINS AND HAS BEEN TRAPPED INSIDE OF

YOUR HEAD AND I AM STILL TRAPPED INSIDE OF IT"
Who Are you" Asked John. "I HAVE GONE BY MANY
NAMES, BUT I AM ONE OF THE PRIMORDIAL GODS OF
CHAOS. EONS AGO ONE OF MY BRETHREN TRAPPED ME
INSIDE OF THIS STONE, NOW I AM TRAPPED INSIDE OF
YOU. I CAN HELP YOU JOHN." "What makes you think I need
help?" inquired John. "BECAUSE I KNOW WHAT YOU WANT,
I CAN GIVE YOU YOUR LEGS BACK, AND SO MUCH
MORE" John was interested but cautious. "What's the catch?
What do you want?" demanded John. "ALL I NEED IS FOR YOU
TO FEED ME YOUR ANGER, FEED ME YOU RAGE. THE
MORE YOU FEED ME THE MORE POWERFUL I CAN
BECOME TO HELP YOU. I AM THE GOD OF CHAOS
REMEMBER." John begins to be filled with pride which fuels
Abraxas, "I am the best officer this city has produced in years I
deserve to be with my partner" thought John. "Besides, I'm already
stuck with this thing why not take advantage of its abilities." "SO,
DO WE HAVE A DEAL?" …. "We can work together now, but
only long enough for me to, eventually, find a way to get you out
of my head safely." John became full of pride and began to stand,

his legs felt stronger than they had ever felt before. "EVEN WITH YOUR DISABILITIES, WHEN YOU USE MY POWERS, YOU WILL BECOME MORE THAN HUMAN," said Abraxas. "I feel amazing" Said John, "better than I have ever felt in years." "AS LONG AS WE STAY IN SYNC AND OUR BOND GROWS, SO WILL YOUR ABILITY TO CONTROL MY POWERS," said Abraxas. "SO, WHAT IS THE FIRST THING THAT YOU WOULD LIKE TO DO? John thinks to himself, recently he has been hearing news of mutants and various attacks on the city. He has felt helpless to do anything about any of it due to his injuries. "We need to figure out what's really going on in this city, if what you are saying is true then we need to put a stop to the mutants and the Demons that are trying to take over my city," John said feeling proud of himself. "I need you to tell me everything about the organization that was trying to free you from the Stone, it's our only lead, we need to start there." Said John. "VERY WELL, THE ORGANIZATION YOU ARE LOOKING FOR IS THE VERY GOVERNMENT THAT YOU USED TO WORK FOR, EVERYTHING THAT YOU THINK YOU KNOW ABOUT THEM IS WRONG. THEY HAVE BEEN MANIPULATING

THEIR SOLDIERS AND THEY HIDE THEIR TRUE AGENDA.

THE GOVERNMENT AND MANY BRANCHES OF IT'S

HEIARCHY HAS BEEN INFILTRATED BY DARK FORCES.

DEMONS ARE IN CONTROL OF ALL THE BRANCHES OF

GOVERNMENT, THEIR AGENDA WAS TO RELEASE ME

AND BRING CHAOS TO THE HUMAN WORLD. YOU AND

YOUR PARTNER MARK GOT TOO CLOSE AND THAT'S

THE TRUTH OF WHY THEY LET YOU GO." Said Abraxas.

John is taken back by the information that he is being given, how

could this be? "What about Mark, is he a part of this?" asked John.

"I'M NOT SURE, I HAVE NEVER WORKED WITH HIM, BUT

DURING MY TIME IN THE STONE I HAVE WORKED WITH

MANY GOVERNMENT AGENTS THAT ATTEMPTED TO

GAIN ACCES TO MY POWERS. EVENTUALY THE

DIRECTOR SUGGESTED THAT THE STONE WAS

DESTROYED THEN THERE WOULD BE A CHANCE THAT I

COULD BE FREED, HE OFFERED HIS BODY TO ME IF I

ESCAPED." This information began to anger John as he thought

about how he had been manipulated. "I need to verify this

information for myself before I accuse the agency of this crime, but if it's true they will all pay for their actions. "John boasted.

"How do I contact these demons?" John asked. "YOU NEED TO FIND SOMEONE WHO HAS THE DEMON SIGIL, THEY ARE THE ONLY ONES WHO CAN SUMMON A DEMON TO THIS WORLD, THEY ARE USUALLY HUMAN WITH A CONNECTION TO THE DARK ARTS." John thinks to himself, "The best place to start should be exactly where I left off, I need to go back to the headquarters and see if I can find out any information. Maybe there are some files that I can search and find more information about what the hell is really going on in the Government" John thinks to himself. "IF YOU RETURN TO THE GOVERNMENT HEADQUARTERS YOU WILL FIND MORE THAN JUST A FILE WITH INFORMATION. THE "EVENT" HAS STARTED AND AT THIS VERY MOMENT THE GOVERNMENT HAS BEEN OVERRUN BY DEMONS AND MUTANTS. BUT THIS WAS THE PLAN, TO MAKE THE ENTIRE THING SEEM LIKE AN ACCIDENT. IT'S BEING KEPT SECRET NOW, BUT NOT FOR LONG, THE GOVERNMENT PLANS TO MUTATE THE ENTIRE POPULATION OF THE PLANET, SO THEY HAVE AN

EXCUSE TO ERRADICATE BILLIONS IN ORDER TO

JUSTIFY POPULATION CONTROL." John hears this and

becomes furious, let us go Abraxas!"

"JOHN, WITH MY POWERS MANY OF YOUR NATURAL HUMAN ABILITIES HAVE BEEN ENHANCED, TRY USING YOUR LEGS TO RUN TO YOUR DESTINATION, YOU SHOULD BE ABLE TO TRAVEL FASTER THAN THE MACHINES THAT YOUR KIND RELYS ON SO MUCH TO SURVIVE." Said Abraxas. "Well here goes nothing" said John to himself. As soon as he began to run, he did not realize how fast he was moving. "YOU NEED TO BE CAUTIOUS WHEN RUNNING FOR EXTENDED PERIODS OF TIME. YOU ARE STILL HUMAN AND YOUR BODY ISN'T DESIGNED TO CONTAIN LIMITLESS POWERS OF THE GODS. YOUR BODY WILL BURN ENERGY AT AN INCREASED RATE THE MORE YOU USE MY POWERS YOU ARE RISKING YOUR VERY LIFE. YOU NEED TO FIND A WAY TO KEEP YOUR ENERGY LEVELS HIGH," said Abraxas. John thought to himself, I need to maintain a reasonable speed that my body can handle, and I need to eat. That is not a problem. MY POWERS CAN PUSH YOUR BODY TO THE SPEED OF SOUND AND FASTER, BUT THE G-FORCES ALONE WOULD CRUSH

YOU. ALTHOUGH YOU ARE ENHANCED BY MY POWER, YOU ARE STILL HUMAN REMEMBER THAT. John slows down to about 250 mph, a comfortable speed for his body size. "At this speed it's still going to take some time to get to the city" John thinks, "I wonder what's going on there?" BEFORE YOU GET THERE YOU NEED TO GAIN AN UNDERSTANDING OF YOUR ABILITIES, NOT ONLY DO YOU HAVE THE ABILITY TO RUN AT INCREDIBLE SPEEDS YOU CAN ALSO CREATE INSTANT HEAT AROUND YOUR FIST AND IF CONCENTRATED YOU MAYBE ABLE YOU RELEASE A HEAT WAVE AND IF YOU BODY CAN TAKE IT YOUR ENTIRE BODY COULD BECOME CONSUMED WITH MY POWERS AND FOR A SHORT PERIOD OF TIME YOU COULD ESSENTIALLY BECOME THE EMBODYMENT OF THE GOD OF CHAOS. THIS TRANSFORMATION COULD KILL YOU, BUT IF TIMES ARE DESPERATE AND YOU NEED TO RELEASE MY FULL POWER IT IS AT YOUR DISPOSAL." said Abraxas. John thinks to himself. "You know demon, I'm not handicapped without your full powers, if you keep my legs working, I don't need to rely on your full abilities. I'm the best officer this city has ever produced, I'll show you what I can do." Abraxas smiles on the inside as he continues to absorb the energy being released from his host. "I JUST LOVE THAT ATTITUDE OF YOURS" said Abraxas to John. John smiled to himself; he knows what the demon wants but he needs to use him before he takes control. Eventually, he knows he may not be able to contain the powers of the demon, but for now he needs to maintain control of his abilities long enough to clean the city up from this disaster, and hopefully separate himself safely from this thing. "Mark probably needs my help and I promised I'd always be there for him." John says aloud. "WHAT IS IT WITH YOU TWO?" asks Abraxas. John thinks to himself and then responds, "I respect him". "YOU MEAN YOU RESENT HIM," said abraxas. "No, what I mean is, I'm trying to understand him." John continues "He had it all, a loving and supporting family, he was top of his class and every university wanted him. All-around athlete, he can be charming, and he is highly intelligent." John pauses. "SO, WHATS THE PROBLEM THEN?" John responds, "I don't know what motivates him to be as good as he is." John begins to get angry; Abraxas takes the chance to absorb all the anger that he can as John begins to rant. "I had NOTHING, no one gave a damn about me, I fought to survive, I figured out life with no help and I earned my place to be among the elite. Maybe I was born with less, but I did not let it stop me, I made it as one of the best officers this city has ever produced." John tries to calm down, but Abraxas instigates the anger further. "…AND WHAT HAS THIS TO DO WITH MARK, I STILL DO NOT UNDERSTAND HUMAN, TELL ME MORE." angrily John continues, "So why is he a fucking officer? he could have done anything with his life, but he wants to run the streets with the low lives like me." John gets angrier and his speed increases, but he is not aware he continues. "The city loves this fool, do you know how many times I had to save his ass on our missions, he has no street smarts, always by the book, but they never want to recognize me. I exceed their expectations; they cannot deny me. I work harder than Mark, and he is just naturally good at everything so I will not let him show me up, I am the only officer that even holds a candle when it comes to matching his skills, he knows I am the only officer that could take him down. That's why I try to protect him." John pauses to calm down but Abraxas pushes on. "IF HE IS SO TALENTED

THEN WHY DOES HE NEED YOUR PROTECTION" John

begins to calm down as he thinks of Mark and the respect, he has

for him despite the anger that grows in his heart. "Because this city

deserves him, he's who I would be if I were in his shoes, he's my

motivation, and when I fight beside him he doesn't treat me like a

loser, he expects the best from me, he expects the best from

everyone, traits like that are rare and needs to be protected, he's so

naïve, he doesn't see the great evils in this world but I do, I feel

like Mark is my purpose, I am his guardian. He is the only thing

that makes sense in my life." John calms down as he realizes that

they are getting nearer to the city. "We are here" John says to

Abraxas. "My body feels like it's on fire, why is that?" Johns asks.

"MOVING AT HIGH RATES OF SPEED WILL CHARGE

YOUR HEAT ABILITIES, YOU GENERATED A LOT OF

POWER WITH YOUR DISPLAY OF ANGER AS YOU WERE

VENTING, YOU NEED TO DISPURSE THAT ADDITIONAL

ENERGY, YOU HAVE NOT USED IT UP. YOU ARE HUMAN

YOUR CAN ONLY STORE SO MUCH ENERGY, IF YOU

OBSORB TOO MUCH ENERGY AND YOU DON'T DISPUSE

IT IN TIME, OR IF YOU RELEASE TOO MUCH OF YOUR

ENERGY AT ONCE YOU RISK THE CHANGE OF PASSING OUT FROM THE SHEER PRESSURE OF USING MY POWERS. I WARNED YOU THAT USING MY POWERS CAME WITH CONSEQUENSES, I WILL SAY AGAIN USE IT WISELY. John begins to remove his clothes due to the temperature of his body increasing. "Your energy is so heavy and so hot" John says. "CALM DOWN I SENSE THAT WE ARE NOT ALONE, THERE SEEMS TO BE A PATROL OF MUTANT CREATURES OUTSIDE OF THE CITY GUARDING THE BORDERS. YOU NEED TO TAKE THEM OUT IF YOU ARE TO COMPETE YOUR MISSION, HERE IS YOUR CHANCE TO RELEASE SOME OF THAT ENERGY." Said Abraxas. John looks in the distance and sees five disfigured and mutated figures near the road that leads into Green Pond City. "Can't we go around" asked John "I was thinking something a little stealthier and quieter. "I AM THE GOD OF CHAOS AND NUCLEAR FIRE; STEALTH IS NOT WHAT I Am GOOD AT. BESIDES, YOU NEED TO RELEASE THAT ENERGY SOON OR YOU WILL PASS OUT. DON'T WORRY I'LL SHOW YOU HOW TO DO IT THE FIRST TIME. LEARN TO CONTROL

THE POWER DO NOT LET IT CONTROL YOU. FOCUS ON WHERE YOU WANT THIS FEELING OF HEAT TO BUILD UP, FOCUS ON YOUR FIST." John begins to concentrate on the heat and moves the powers from his body to his hands. His hands felt enormously hot, but they were not being harmed. "NO MATTER HOW HOT IT FEELS MY POWERS WILL NEVER BURN YOU, AS A MATTER OF FACT YOU CONTROL HOW HOT YOU WANT YOUR HEAT TO BURN. YOU CAN STOP IT ALL IN AN INSTANT, MY POWERS WILL OBEY YOUR COMMANDS." Said Abraxas. "Well, that's good to know", Said John as he sighed relief. "So, what now?" asks John. "WE ATTACK QUICKLY IF DONE CORRECTLY MAYBE YOU CAN STILL HAVE YOUR STEALTH AFTERALL. BECAUSE NOW THAT YOU HAVE MOVED YOUR POWERS TO YOUR HANDS, THEY WILL BEGIN NATURALLY RELEASING HEAT AND POWER INTO THE SURROUNDING ATMOSHERE UNTIL THE HEAT IS ALL DISAPPATED, IF THAT HAPPENS THEN YOU MUST CHARGE YOUR ENERGIES AGAIN AND REPEAT THE PROCESS. IF YOU MISS YOUR WINDOW OF SURPRISE HERE YOU MAY NOT

HAVE TIME TO RECHARGE YOUR ANGER AND YOUR

ENERGIES. WHEN YOU ARE ANGRY DO NOT WASTE IT,

HUMAN EMOTIONS ARE WEAK AND THEY DO NOT LAST

LONG, TAKE ADVANTAGE WHILE THE ABILITIES ARE

AVAILIBLE TO YOU." John thinks to himself, "this is a lot to

take in, but I can handle it. "ONE MORE THING" interrupts

Abraxas. John sighs "Damn, there is more, spit it out already."

"WHEN YOUR HANDS ARE CHARGED THEY CAN EITHER

RELEASE ALL OF THE STORED ENERGY AT ONCE IN A

VERY POWERFULY BUT SHORT RANGED HEAT WAVE,

VIBRATING ALL OF THE SURROUNDING ATOMS IN THE

ATMOSPHERE AT SUCH A FAST RATE THAT

TEMPUATURES CAN BECOME HOT ENOUGH TO MELT

STEEL AND HOTTER, BUT THIS COULD POTENTUALLY

DRAIN ALL OF YOUR POWERS TO QUICKLY AND YOU

COULD LOSE CONSCIENCE BUT YOU WILL CERTAINLY

KILL YOUR ENEMY, OR YOU COULD USE YOUR SPEED

TO GET CLOSE FOR A PHYSICAL ATTACK AND

INCREASE THE POWER OF YOUR PUNCHES WITH

NUCLEAR HEAT ITS ENOUGH TO DEFEAT MANY

WEAKER ENEMIES WITH ONLY ONE HIT." Abraxas

concludes, "I WILL ALLOW YOU TO DISCOVERY SOME OF

MY OTHER POWERS ON YOUR OWN, I COULD SPEND

THE REST OF ETERNITY TELLING YOU OF ALL THE

THING YOU COULD BE CAPABLE OF, BUT MOST OF IT

WOULD KILL YOU." John nods in agreement, "You are doing

both of us a favor buddy, I'm not the one to really listen to lessons,

I make my own rules anyway, but that was a nice tutorial, now let

me show you why I'm the best officer this city has ever produced."

John fills himself with pride and charges his hands that the sheer

weight alone is incredible. "I've got to time this just right" John

says as he begins to charge forward, his first target already in

sights. "HERE WE GO ABRAXAS", yells Johns as he speeds off

into battle.

FAST FORWARD

John decides that overwhelming the enemy with speed would be the best plan of action since he is outnumbered five to one. He does not have any backup; he does not have any protective gear and he is still a novice at using his newly found weapons. But if he hits them fast and hard, they may not get up and continue the fight, which would be ideal when John is in such a rush anyway. I have got to time this exactly right. Filled with pride, John charges into battle and rams his first target; the inertia from the attack throws the mutant off balance and catches the other mutants off guard. His plan seems to be working, the first mutant is not getting up. John rushes towards the second, and then immediately towards the third. At his speed, the mutants were not able to see what was attacking them, but they had become aware of his presence. The mutants vigilantly scanned the area trying to detect the unseen threat. As John rushed towards his third target, he was suddenly stopped in his tracks upon impact with the mutant. This mutant had a body made completely of stones and rocks; it was like running into a brick wall. The impact knocked John to the ground and made him quite dizzy for a moment. During this time, the mutants noticed him and the last remaining three mutants began to come towards him as he tried to shake the dizziness off. "GET YOURSELF UP HUMAN, THE MUTANTS ARE ABOUT TO KILL YOU, PREPARE TO DEFEND YOURSELF BECAUSE YOUR ELEMENT OF SURPRISE ATTCK DIDN'T WORK" said Abraxas to John. John begins standing on his feet as he clears his head. "Yea I know, one of them caught me off guard, I did not know these things could become inorganic, I should have done some recon before the attack, Mark would have suggested that. You know, you are a lousy partner." John said to himself scolding Abraxas for his lack of information on the targets. "Listen, If I die then you die Demon, remember that your number one priority is to protect my life and your life" John said continuing his scolding of his parasitic partner. "I AM SORRY AND I WILL TRY TO DO BETTER, THIS IS A NEW EXPERIENCE FOR ME, I HAVE NEVER HAD TO SHARE MY POWERS BEFORE AND NORMALLY SUCH CREATURES WOULD BE MERE CHILDREN TOYS TO ME IN MY TRUE FORM, BUT I AM LIMITED TO THE WEAKNESSES OF THE HUMAN BODY, I DIDN'T THINK THAT THE MUTANT WOULD BE A

PROBLEM FOR MY POWERS." Abraxas explained defensively. "The mutant is literally a living ROCK; did you really think I could just run right through him?" John scolded "YES, I DID" answered Abraxas "BUT NEVER MIND THAT, WHAT DO YOU PLAN TO DO ABOUT YOUR INCOMING ATTACKERS." Shaking off the collision John looks around to see his attacker quickly approaching, three mutants each seem a bit unique in their own way. "What can you tell me about each of them?" John asks Abraxas. "I AM ABLE TO SENSE THEIR ENERGY, THE FIRST IS THE ROCK MUTANT HIS BODY APPEARS TO BE PURLY STONE, YOU NEED TO HIT HIM HARD ENOUGH IN ORDER TO BREAK THE STONES AND DAMAGE HIM, TRY TO AVOID HIM FOR NOW, WE NEED TO FOCUS OUR ENERGY ON TAKING OUT THE OTHER TWO FIRST, ONE APPEARS TO BE ABLE TO MORPH HIS HANDS INTO DIFFERENT TYPES OF WEAPONS, BUT HIS BODY SEEMS TO STILL BE ORGANIC MEANING ORDINARY ATTACKS CAN HURT HIM. THE FINAL HAS THE ABILITY TO CAMOUFLAGE HIMSELF INTO HIS ENVIORMENT, NOT JUST FOR ILLUSION, HE CAN

BECOME WHATEVER ENVIORNMENT HE ENTERS. I

SUGGEST WE TAKE HIM OUT SECOND, READY

YOURSELF HERE THEY COME." Trying to remember all the

lessons Abraxas had taught him so far, he prepares himself as the

first mutant to emerge, the other two can be heard fast

approaching. The Mutant attacks quickly, turning his hand into a

giant hammer. He smashes the ground near John, nearly crushing

him, but John dodges the attack quickly. The Mutant quickly

changes his other hand into a large axe and swings it at John.

"NOW IS YOUR CHANCE, ATTACK HIM QUICKLY BEFORE

HE RECOVERS AND CHANGES HIS FORM INTO

SOMETHING ELSE, AND BESIDES, YOU HAVE TWO MORE

TO DEAL WITH YOU CAN'T WASTE TIME HERE, FINISH

HIM QUICKLY, NOW! John fills himself with pride, excited to

be walking again, let alone running and fighting, he rushes towards

the mutant with great speed and from multiple angles launch a

barrage of well time and well-placed nuclear charges strikes to the

creature's body and head. The mutant attempts one last attack and

flails his arms wildly while randomly changing each arm into

different weapons, simply attacking everywhere it can, John, however, is simply too fast for his attack. Continuing his pattern of dodging and striking with precision, the creature is overwhelmed and finally collapses to the ground, after receiving over 200 punches and kicks withing less than 20 seconds. John was warned that prolonged use of Abraxas powers will have a negative effect on his energy levels and can eventually take a toll on his body, he begins to feel exhausted himself. He takes a second to try and catch his breath. "NO, YOU DO NOT HAVE TIME TO REST NOW HUMAN, THE OTHER MUTANT IS SOMEWHERE NEAR YOU" John is panting heavily as he tries to catch his breath. "I know, but I'm tired, it's really heavy carrying you around in my body, and I just hit this guy like two-hundred times, I need a second." John says breathing heavily. "YOU DO NOT HAVE A SECOND" Abraxas said. At that moment, the ground begins to move and shake opening and trapping Johns legs in the earth. "What's going on?" John asks, taken by surprise. "IT'S THE MUTANT HE HAS BECOME THE GROUND AND HE HAS YOU TRAPPED, I WARNED YOU TO BE ON YOUR GUARD." Said Abraxas. "Don't worry I'll improvise, I'm sure we will think of something." Just as John finishes his sentence, the rock creature approaches very fast and seeing that John is trapped swings his large rocklike arms and knocks John Backwards uprooting him from the ground, the impact send John soaring through the air and tumbling on the ground before he comes crashing into a tree, a bit dizzy but otherwise ok John jokes "Hey at least we are free" "I WOULDN'T BE SO SURE ABOUT THAT" Abraxas warns as the very tree that they were leaning on begins to move and wrap it's branches around John. The mutant had become the tree, they were trapped again. "Damn, I spoke too soon," said John. "WELL, ONCE AGAIN THAT'S WHAT I WAS TRYING TO WARN YOU ABOUT." Abraxas explains. "THE ROCK CREATURE IS APPROACHING FAST AND WE CANNOT CONTINUE TO TAKE HIS ATTACKS WITHOUT AFFECT. REMEMBER YOU ARE HUMAN," Johns gets a little nervous "What should I do?" He asks Abraxas. "CONCENTRATE ALL OF MY ENERGY INTO YOUR HANDS LIKE I SHOWED YOU BEFORE BUT THIS TIME DO NOT RELEASE IT JUST ALLOW IT TO VIBRATE AND DISPURSE THROUGHOUT THE AIR AROUND YOU. CREATE A GIANT MICROWAVE EFFECT." John focuses and Abraxas release an enormous amount of energy into the air heating the surrounding area until it becomes hot enough to at least boil water. The tree mutant passes out immediately as the temperature rises nearly boiling his blood, His camouflage is released as he falls to the ground in flames, Abraxas continues increasing the temperature of the heat wave as the rock mutant enters the perimeters of the expanded heat wave. The temperatures have risen to hot enough to melt stone. Once the rock creature enters too close to John, he immediately regrets it as his limbs begin melting and falling off due to the extreme temperatures within the area near John, the mutant tries to escape but ended up being a large pile of hot molten rock and lava, melted by the extreme heats of the Chaos God. Abraxas begins to rescind the heat and retract it back into himself. "I'm not feeling so well" said John as he begins to fall to the ground completely exhausted now. He remembers using too much of the GODS powers can leave you weak and vulnerable possibly unconscious and helpless.

"YOU NEED TO EAT AND REST; NO HUMAN HAS EVER BEEN ABLE TO CONTROL THE POWERS OF A GOD FOR THIS LONG WITHOUT THE AFFECTS. REST FOR NOW UNTIL WE CAN GET TO FOOD, WE WILL GET THERE

SOON." John releases his body and gives in to his exhaustion, he was asleep and desperately needed the rest, but at least he was safe, he thought as he dozed off.

REUNION

Slowly John opens his eyes and tries to gather himself. He pulls himself to his feet and stretches looking around to survey his immediate surroundings, he stays true to his training. "How long was I out?" John asks, "IT APPEARS YOU WERE SLEEPING FOR ABOUT TWO DAYS, NEARLY 48 HOURS" answers Abraxas, "Wow, I have never slept that long, and I feel hungry" John replies. "YOU STILL NEED TO EAT SOMETHING BEFORE YOU CAN REGAIN YOUR FULL STREGNTH, BUT BECAUSE OF YOUR REST YOU HAVE ENOUGH ENERGY TO ACCESS MY POWERS BUT AS ALWAYS BE CAUSTIOUS." Warned Abraxas. "Yea, I know, I've got this, I'll be fine" John said arrogantly. After a good stretch John continues his journey into the city to investigate current events and the claims that Abraxas had informed him about the Government and the Agency that he worked for. Mostly he worried if Mark was doing Okay during all this chaos. As John enters the city, he sees that there is more destruction than he would have believed. Only a few miles away no one even knows what is going on in this city. "This is unbelievable, the city is completely overrun, and no one has even signaled for help" John says, surprisingly. "PAY

CLOSER ATTENTION JOHN, THE MUTANTS COULD HAVE

ESCAPED AND BEGUN TO ATTACK OTHER AREAS BUT

THAT'S NOT WHAT THEY WANT. THEY ARE

PROTECTING SOMETHING. THEY ARE TRYING TO KEEP

PEOPLE OUT." Abraxas advises John. "You are right" John says,

"this is not just some random accident this seems more like a

coordinated terrorist attack." John says. "IM NOT SURE WHO IS

RESPONSIBLE FOR THIS BUT IM SURE THAT IF YOU CAN

MAKE IT TO THE GOVERNMENT COMPOUND CLOSER TO

THE GREEN POND THAT YOU WILL FIND THE ANSWERS

THAT YOU SEEK." Throughout the city many of the mutants

seem to not even notice as John sneaks about in short speed burst

making his way to the center of the city towards the large

Government complex that surrounds the famous Green Pond. "It

seems that many of these creatures are harmless, not nearly as

aggressive as the ones I fought before. They do not seem to pose

any immediate threat. Anyone trained in law enforcement can tell

when they are in a threatening situation and these creatures seem

docile." Johns says continuing to observe his surroundings. "I

NOTICED THAT BUT I WOULD STILLWARN YOU TO BE VIGILANT YOU DO NOT KNOW WHEN OR IF THEY WILL BECOME HOSTILE, STAY DEFENSIVE." warns Abraxas "agreed" said John more determined to get to the bottom of this. Finally, the government facility is in sight and John just needs to find a way inside. "There are large mutants everywhere the compound is completely surrounded." John says. "YOU DO NOT HAVE ENOUGH ENERGY FOR A FULL-SCALE ASSAULT, ALTHOUGH YOU RESTED, UNLESS YOU FULL REPLENISH YOUR ENERGY WITH FOOD YOU WILL NOT LAST LONG IN A BATTLE USING MY POWERS. IF YOU ARE DISCOVERED YOU CAN EITHER ESCAPE OR YOU ARE ON YOUR OWN WITH YOUR NATURAL ABILITIES UNTIL YOU CAN RECHARGE." John thinks about his situation and tries to figure out the best way inside the complex. "What if we create a diversion and then sneak in that way" John says asking Abraxas for confirmation. "THAT MAY WORK BUT HOW DO YOU WANT TO CREATE IT." asked Abraxas. "I'm still working on that one" John answers. Suddenly to both of their surprise there was a large explosion near the rear of the compound and what sounded like gunfire. "Someone is fighting back there; do you hear that?" Said John "WE CAN USE THIS," said Abraxas. "Agreed" said John. Many of the mutants begin to charge towards the back of the complex leaving the front nearly completely unguarded. "They are not too smart" said John jokingly as he makes his way towards the front gate and into the complex. "LET'S TRY TO STAY AS FAR AWAY FROM THE REAR OF THE COMPLEX AS POSSIBLE TO AVOID UNNESSESARY COMBAT." Abraxas advised. "Agreed" John said rushing towards the entrance of one of the first buildings of the Government complex. "Our mission is to find information that will validate your claim that the Government is behind all of this." John says. "I BELIEVE YOU WILL FIND MORE THAN THAT BUT I WILL LET YOU DECIDE FOR YOURSELF." said Abraxas confidently. John proceeds to enter and scarch the first building, everything seemed normal. John continued to search the second and the third buildings until there was only the main building remaining. "So far no luck Demon, I have only found military records, medical files and loosely classified mission information but nothing that even remotely justifying your claim." John says, feeling doubtful and used. "YOUR SEARCH IS NOT OVER HUMAN, AND REMEMBER, I AM A GOD, I AM MORE POWERFUL THAN A MERE DEMON, ONCE YOU FIND WHAT YOU SEEK YOU WILL BE GRATEFUL THAT YOU LISTENED TO ME." Abraxas says, confirming and confidently validating his own claim. John pushed forward and approached the main building. Although the building is surrounded by a thick wall, John uses his frustration to power himself enough to melt a hole into the cement wall and enter the courtyard. There are only a few human guards, it seems nearly abandoned. "REMEMBER NO COMBAT YOU CANNOT USE MY POWERS TOO MUCH.' Warned Abraxas. John uses just a little speed to sneak past the few guards and into the front door of the main building. "This is almost too easy" John whispers to himself, "PROCEED CAUTIOUSLY TO THE RESEARCH ROOM" Abraxas advises. John creeps through the facility room by room and instantly searching each for any clues to validate the insane voice inside of his head. As John approaches the research room, he is unaware that he is being tracked and followed. Abraxas senses the presence of someone else and warns John. "Be careful, I sense that someone else is here watching you."

warns Abraxas. Before John could react, the lights in the facility went out. A voice cried out from the darkness. "I do not know why you are here, but you will regret every second that you have invaded this classified facility." The voice sounds familiar to John. "Mark" John thinks to himself. Suddenly, smoke and gas are released in the immediate area, the doors are locked, and John is trapped, he cannot see, and he begins to cough from the smoke and gas being released "WHOEVER HE IS HE IS VERY CLEVER, NOT ONLY HAS HE BLOCKED YOUR LINE OF SIGHT SO THAT YOU CAN'T FIND HIM, BUT HE HAS ALSO FOUND A WAY FOR YOU TO GIVE YOUR POSITION AWAY, NOT ALLOWING YOU TO HIDE FROM HIM." said Abraxas, sounding impressed by this human's battle tactics. John tries to speak but he cannot stop coughing, trying to catch his breath as the gas fills the room. "Is there nothing that you can do to help me Demon?" asks John as he struggles to catch his breath and look for an escape route out of the building and the gas. "IF IT WERE ME, I WOULD BLOW UP THE ENTIRE BUILDING WITH MY POWERS BUT YOU ARE NOT STRONG ENOUGH NOW TO USE THEM. YOUR ONLY CHANGE IS TO TRY TO ESCAPE."

John continues to cough and give away his hiding position as he scans the room for a way out, but before he can even react, he feels a slight pinch on the back of his shoulder. "YOU HAVE BEEN TAGGED WITH A TRANQUILIZER DART; IT SEEMS LIKE HE IS TRYING TO CAPTURE YOU." John begins to panic which diminished his abilities from the chaos god. He tries to use his speed to rush towards the door but as soon as he moves, he runs directly into a trap. Tripwires have been placed all along the floor and not only does he fall to the ground, but his legs are quickly bound and wrapped by a strong steel rope. "I noticed that you have the ability to run at incredible speed." The voice says from the darkness, muffled a little bit by what can obviously be a gas mask protecting him from the smoke and gas mixture. "You have been on our cameras since you entered this government complex and you underestimate our defenses, big mistake." The voice continues. John lies on the ground and continues to cough, his feet tied together his powers are gone, and the dart in his back is starting to take effect. There is no use fighting it anymore, he has lost this fight. John lies in wait for his attacker to emerge. Slowly, a figure in a gas mask and tactical suit begins walking towards

John as he begins to pass out, he tries to see if he can recognize him, weakly John speaks "Mark, is that you?... The tranquilizer and gas finally take effect and John once again falls unconscious. As the figure gets closer the gas starts to dissipate and the figure walks closer to John so that he can have a good look at this invader, and to his surprise he recognizes him. "JOHN!" yells the voice out loud as the figure turns out to indeed be Johns ex-Partner turned special agent Mark Jones.

REVALATIONS

"John, wake up sweetie, come on we need to begin your lessons today, John… John…" John opens his eyes and sees sister Mary, one of the sisters from the church that he was raised. "Wait, how are you here, am I dreaming?" John questions what he sees, knowing that sister Mary along with the other members of the church all died in a fire years ago when he was 17 years old. Sister Mary found John, left at the Alter of the church as a baby. He never knew his parents, so sister Mary became his adopted mother and Father John, who he was named after became his adopted father. John follows sister Mary, knowing that she cannot be real, this must be a dream from my past. "Where are we going" John asks, "you are late for your lessons today" answered sister Mary "Father John would be upset if he knew you were sleeping through your lessons" John walks down the hall of the old church "I remember this place" thinks John to himself as he enters a classroom and sees a younger version of himself sitting at a desk and barley paying attention to the teacher who was pointing to something on the blackboard. Sister Mary waits at the door as John walks closer to hear what the teacher is trying to tell him. There is a picture of a creature on the blackboard, John gets closer to see what it is, and the voice of the teacher becomes clear. "John, if you ever come across this entity remember do not trust him, for he is the Demon of Chaos and he feeds off the life force of the living to make him stronger." John looks at his younger self, who was not paying attention and could care less about what was being told to him. There is a name written and John approaches to get a better look at who this creature is, he looks back at sister Mary who is smiling and encouraging him to have a look. Suddenly John is taken back when he sees the name "ABRAXAS!!" He looks at sister Mary with a terrified look on his face, but she is still smiling, "Now wake up John, wake up… John…John…John… the voice begins to fade away. "JOHN! JOHN! WAKE UP THIS IS NO TIME TO BE SLEEPING!" Yells ABRAXAS as John begins to slowly open his eyes and the effects of the tranquilizer fades. John remembers where he is, but he still feels weak. He hears voices in the background talking, and notices that he is strapped down on a table laying on his back. "ARE YOU FINALLY AWAKE NOW SLEEPING BEAUTY" teases ABRAXAS as John tries to compose himself. He hears Mark talking to someone behind him and he tries to listen. "So, do you know who this person is?" asked the unfamiliar voice. "Yes, he is my ex-partner, but it makes no sense because he lost the ability to walk, he retired from duty" Mark answers "So what is he doing here in the city, and how did he get into a classified facility." The voice asks, "I don't know, but he doesn't seem to be mutated like the others, so I don't want to kill him." answered Mark. "Then you need to find out what he wants and why is he here." The voices scolds Mark. "There was an attack at the back of the compound, and we have others in an interrogation room trying to find out what they know and why they are here also. They are not mutated, and I need to speak with them. You take care of this and when he wakes bring him in the room with the others." The voice walks out of the room. Mark looks over at John and notices that he is fidgeting. "So, you are finally awake I see." Mark says as he approaches John. John moans "why am I tied up, Mark" Mark answers with a question, "John what are you doing here, and How is it possible that you can walk again?" Mark continues, "You were once government, you know that certain information is classified from civilians, you could have been killed." John begins to get angry, and this feeds Abraxas, "What do you mean Mark, there are MUTANTS running the streets

everywhere, the city is a ghost town, I came to find out what's

going on here. The truth Mark, what is the Government up to?"

John asks angrily. Mark lowers his head, "that's classified John,

but come with me maybe once we meet up with the others the

director can explain things better than I can." Mark says. "LET'S

GO ALONG WITH HIM FOR NOW, BECAUSE I SENSE THE

PRESENCE OF OTHER LIFE FORMS LIKE ME NEARBY,

THIS MAY GET DEEPER THAN I PREDICTED" Abraxas says

to John. "I agree, and after that little rest I feel fully recharged."

John says to himself as Mark begins to release the restraints. "WE

ARE AT FULL POWER JOHN, ALL OF MY POWERS ARE

AVAILIBLE TO YOU AGAIN, RMEMEBER TO BE CAREFUL

WITH THEM, YOU NEED TO CONTINUE TO REST WHEN

YOU DO NOT NEED THE POWERS AND EAT EVERY

CHANCE YOU CAN." Warns Abraxas. "Yea, I got it I got it"

says John to himself as the final restraints are released and he hops

off the table standing to his feet. "It's a Miracle", laughs Mark as

he approaches John with a file dossier in his hands. "What's this?"

asks John as he reaches for the file. "You should read it, things will begin to come clear for you soon" Mark pauses "Seriously, how are you walking again, I thought you were disabled?" Mark asks curiously. "LIE TO HIM JOHN, DO NOT REVEAL THE SOURCE OF YOUR POWER TO HIM YET, WE STILL CANNOT TRUST HIM" warns Abraxas. Without hesitation John replies, "Honestly I'm not sure what the doctors did, but somehow with enough money, I am able to walk again" John answers with a lie as Abraxas instructed. "GOOD JOB JOHN, IF YOU CONTINUE TO FOLLOW MY WORDS, I PROMISE YOU THAT THE ENTIRE PLAN WILL PLAY ITSELF OUT AND YOU WILL FINALLY KNOW THE TRUTH". Abraxas says excitedly as John begins to read the file dossier and follow Mark down the hall to meet the director with the rest of the visitors.

GUARDIANS OF THE NINE LIVES

In ancient times cats were worshipped as GODS; they have not forgotten this".
-Terry Pratchett

"The wildlife in this city is starting to move further and further away. It seems as if there is a great migration going on between multiple species" "I have never seen anything like this sir, there is something wrong. The only time animals act this way is if they sense a natural disaster or danger of some sort. If you want my honest opinion, I think we need to evacuate the city. I don't know what's coming but it cannot be good." The room gets silent. "Do you know what you are saying Angela"," You want the committee to evacuate the city simply based on the fact that some animals are behaving strangely?" The leader of the committee asks. "Yes, Sir, in all my years of study, these behaviors show signs of immediate danger and I think we should move people to a safer area until we know what's really going on. These early warning signs are seen all over the animal kingdom and there is never a doubt that danger comes soon after." The Committee seems to talk among themselves shortly before deciding. "Angela, the committee respects your decision, however the resources needed to do that will take some time. We would like you to continue your research. Try to find out what is happening, we need more details. Also see if you can find out where the animals are going. If we are evacuating the city, we need to know that wherever we go is going to be safe. It's just too early to make that kind of decision without further information." Said the committee leader. "I understand," said Angela. "I will try to find the information that you need." As Angela walks out of the room, she overhears one of the committee leaders speaking to the other about her. "She is one of the greatest wildlife biologists there is, if she says something is coming, I'm sure she is right." Angela Smiles to herself, then the other committee member replies. "We don't yet know enough about what we are dealing with to make any kind of intelligent decision. If she is as good as you say she is, then she will find us the information we need." Angela feels determined now to prove her theory. She knows there is something about to happen, but she cannot find any signs of a natural disaster. That night as she tracks a herd of migrating animals. The herd stopped to get water near the green pond Angela would be able to study the effects of the water on the herd and find out where they were heading. As Angela begin to set up her equipment, a large cat emerged from the nearby woods and attacked the herd killing two of them before the rest escaped. Angela realized that this was an exceedingly rare species of cat, especially this close to the city. She decided to abandon the herd and track the cat. Unknown to her was that the same cat was being tracked by hunters. In amazement Angela photographed and recorded the large cat as he enjoyed his meal. "What are you doing here big fella" Angela said to herself. Suddenly, Angela heard footsteps, and so did the cat, his head lifted, and his ears raised. Angela sat quietly not knowing what it was. Suddenly she heard gunfire and saw the large cat fall. "OH GOD "Thought Angela, as she watched the hunter emerge from the woods and approach the large cat. Tears in her eyes as she mourned silently for the beautiful specimen that had just been massacred in front of her eyes. As the hunters got closer, they realized that the cat was not dead but severely injured. "Hey, this cat isn't dead yet" Exclaimed one of the hunters. "You should have shot him in the head. Here let me finish him so that he doesn't suffer." Angela heard this, and she felt hope that maybe the cat could be saved if only she could plead and beg the hunters not to kill him then she is sure that she can save his life. "WAIT" Angela Screams as she emerges from her hiding spot. "WAIT PLEASE" The three hunters turn to face her. Cautiously she approaches them.

"Please, do not kill this cat, he is exceedingly rare. I am a Wildlife biologist; I have been following this cat before you shot it. If he is still alive there is a chance, I can save it, but you must let it live. PLEASE" Angela pleads with the hunters, but they only laughed at her. "Little girl you are at the wrong place at the wrong time, this cat is worth a lot of money, and we want that money." Said one of the hunters. "No Please," said Angela. "You shouldn't be worried about this cat more than yourself." Said the other hunter "The boss that paid for this job doesn't want any witnesses." He gave Angela a cynical smile. Immediately she knew she was in danger. If she was going to save herself and the life of the cat she had to fight back, as the hunter with the rifle pointed the gun at Angela. She pushed him into the Green Pond, upon falling, he fired and missed Angela but hit one of his partners instead. Before Angela could turn to the third hunter, she was hit on the head and fell unconscious. When she woke, she was tied up to the dying Cat and she heard the hunter say, "since you like this cat so much you can die with him" and he pushed both Angela and the Cat into the Green Pond for a watery death. No One knows how deep the green pond is and it seems that today would-be Angela's last day as she sank down the depths probably never to be found. She held her breath for as long as she could and then, suddenly. Angela inhaled, and nothing happened. Surprisingly, she had sunken into an underwater cavern, there was air but barely. She was still tired and with her strength draining she passed out. While she and the large cat lay in an underwater cavern somewhere under the green pond, the mysterious waters begin to influence the two. The green Pond water is considered TOXIC and the effect it has on everything that touches it is always different. No one has ever been this submerged in the green pond before and the effects are unknown. Angela enters a deep sleep, and the large cat seems to have stopped moving. In Angela's dream she enters the realm of the Cat. Amazed, she seemed to be at a meeting of some sort. There are many enormous cats sitting in a circle surrounding Angela and the dying Cat. "Is this real" Angela asks out loud. "Define real" answered one of the large cats with a thunderous voice. "Where am I, what is going on how is this possible" Demands Angela fearfully. "Calm yourself Human" You are in the judgment, it appears that you and Samson are in a state of passing, and somehow you were transported to the Cat realm instead of the human realm." Said one of the cats. "Samson?" asks Angela. "He is the cat who is dying beside you." Said one of the enormous cats. "It appears that your soul is trapped under the green water, and it cannot leave, we are trying to decide if Samson has anymore of his nine lives but there isn't anything we can do for a human. You are not dead yet, but you are going to die. We can resurrect Samson, but he is trapped under water and a cat of his species cannot get out. It seems we have a dilemma." "Who are you" Angela Asks. "We are the Guardians of the Nine Lives. "Wow Cats have their own GODS", thought Angela. "There seems to be only one solution" The Guardian spoke. "We will combine the souls which give them both the best chance to survive but you must become one of our kind to grant us power over you. Otherwise, you will die human." It appears I have no choice Angela thought. So, she agrees. "You are no longer human, from this moment forward your soul belongs to the guardians of the nine lives. Angela McWaters has died and only the CAT Lives. Now Awaken!"

UNEXPECTED BONDS

The Sunshine through the window and the alarm starts to blare loudly. Angela is laying on her back on the couch in the living room of her apartment. She slowly wakes as she stumbles to her room to turn off the alarm. "Ah my head hurts" says Angela as she turns the alarm off and thinks to herself. "What happened… Was it all a dream? … How did I end up back here, I thought I died" Still feeling weak she stumbles through the house to get to the kitchen. "I need something to drink" as she opens the kitchen door, she notices an enormous cat laying in the middle of the floor. He lifts his head and speaks, "Are you really going into work today?" … "YIKES" screamed Angela startled at the sight of the CAT. The fact that it spoke sent shivers down her spine. "Would you get off the wall and come down here, what's gotten into you," said the cat. "You're a talking CAT," said Angela. "Yea, and you're a human clinging to a wall," said Sam. Until this very moment Angela had not realized that she was hanging from the side of the wall. She had jumped so effortlessly, and the reaction was almost second nature to her. "What the hell" Angela said as she jumped off the wall. Calmer now but still cautious she approached the large cat.

"Hello Angela, I am Sam, and I will be your life partner from here on out, because of what the GUARDIANS did with our souls we've got to protect each other." "Whoa, so it was real screamed Angela" "Quite real, you died and so did I, to save your life you traded your human soul for that of a cat, so the GUARDIANS created you a brand-new soul. Your original soul is probably still trapped somewhere under the green water for some reason it could not leave Every soul needs a body and since your original soul no longer wanted to be Angela McWaters anymore there was an empty vessel. There would be effects to the body now that you have the soul of a cat but inside a human body. On the Outside you are Angela McWaters but, on the inside, you are a cat who shares her nine lives with me." "So, what did you get out of the deal?" Angela Asked. "Well as you can see, I can speak, and I have gained human intelligence and reasoning. It was not intended but we also share MINDS. While you gained access to my remaining 7 lives and the natural abilities of a cat, I already have those, but what I did not have was the human mind, now I do." Angela stood in shock for a bit as her mind processed everything that she was being told and accepting the fact that she died in some sort of way.

But she was given another opportunity to live life. "It's going to be OK Angie," said Sam. "I know this is a lot to take in especially for a human with limited beliefs. There are things about life and death that humans have not discovered yet. With your limited wisdom It is understandable that you would fear death. As you can see there is more to death than you could imagine, but now is not the time to discuss those things. Take some time to get used to your body and the side effects that you are going to experience until your new soul settles inside of this body." Angela was even more surprised at Samson. "Wow, you are very intelligent!" She said, "More than you can imagine," said Sam. At that moment they both noticed the broadcast being played on the TV. "There are reports of numerous mutilated animals that have been found spread throughout Green Pond City" The reporter on the TV announced. "It appears as if their bodied were used to harvest specific animal parts for reason unknown and the remains of these creature were just thrown aside like trash." Angela and Sam looked at each other silently but thinking the exact same thing. The reporter continued. "They all died from Gunshot wounds from hunters, but many of these animals are endangered and illegal to hunt. The Government will be looking for answers, they are calling these killings MURDER!

There is much politics over whether animals have enforceable

rights. Until the government decides, these murders will go

unpunished." Angela Turned the TV Off and Looked at Sam with a

fierce look in her eyes. "LET'S GO SAM!" she demanded.

THE THRILL OF THE HUNT

The news broadcast of a bizarre string of the murder of animals is all over the city as many people morn the heartless actions committed against these creatures. The governments cannot seem to decide how they want to handle the situation, all the while animals are dying. There are no laws that govern these things, besides humans still consume animals as a food source, so it is hard to have sympathy for what is happening. "What do we do first" Sam asked. "Well, the first thing we need to do is find out more information on who these people are." Angela replied. "I heard the hunters say they were looking for rare species of animals, there is some rich guy out there paying for these murders." Angela continued. "The problem is tracking this guy down.". "Well," Sam interrupts, "there might be a way." Sam leaps out the open window and begins climbing the side of the wall. "C'mon" encouraged Sam as he reached the roof Angela's apartment building. Hesitantly, Angela began climbing slowly. Oddly, this felt more natural than she thought. "I was afraid that learning to be a cat would be harder than this." Angela said, surprised at how quickly she had mastered her new abilities. "You must realize that you are already a Cat, so you do not need to learn to be one, all of the abilities I have you have, and you already know how to perform them." Sam explained. So, do not be afraid to let your body move, it knows what it is doing." Angela looked puzzled to hear this but didn't want to discuss it." So, why are we up here?" Angela asked still puzzled. "Because I know a guy, lives on the edge of town near the Green Pond Forest. He is a wild cat, but he feeds off human trash to avoid hunting. He always has news of what is going on in the human world, maybe he has something we can start with." Sam explained. Angela looked even more puzzled than she was before "Wait so you want us to talk to a CAT!!" She said in surprise. "Angie, I am a cat, and so are you. Did you expect me to speak to a human?" Sam chuckled "Can you imagine, me a six-foot cat walking up and speaking to a human?" Sam continued to chuckle. "Angie you are funny." Sam leaps off the building, clings to the wall of the next one and continues towards the forest. Angela watches and she thinks to herself "Angie… I like that" Angela smiles and yells out to Sam. "Hey Wait up." Angela, still a little hesitant with her new abilities, leaps and tries to catch up to Sam. "What were you doing in the forest anyway Angie" Sam asked as he continued. "I was working for the government; I was supposed to be investigating the strange migration of all of the animals." Angela answered. "I saw you and I abandoned my duty because you are such a beautiful and rare cat, I had to track you." Angela continued. That is when I saw the hunters and I begged for your life, but they tried to take mine…" Angela paused and then asked "What were you doing there. Your species of cat is not known to be in these parts of the city near humans." Angela said, curious for an answer. Sam turned back and smirked, then he replied. "So, you thought I was a beautiful cat?! That is nice of you Angie." Angela blushed a little, it is still strange to speak with a cat that has human consciousness and intelligence, also she could not ignore the fact that Sam was an unbelievably beautiful cat, even more so now that she is also a cat. Angela had not paid much attention to where she was going, she had not concerned herself much about who they were meeting and how this would even help her. She followed Sam, unquestionably obedient to his commands. Even now, she finds herself so stunned by his recognition of her attraction to him and his direct acknowledgment of it. His attention to details, his command authority immediately when it is time to react. She wanted to know more about him, and she had completely missed the fact that he dodged her question entirely. Sam took notice of her delay in responding to his deflection, he looked back and again smirked. He watched her do her best to keep up with him as they continued to make their way across the moonlit roof top of green pond city. Angela caught a glimpse of Sam smirking at her and realized what she had done, she frowns and raises her voice in aggravation. "Hey, that's not an answer to my question, I told you what I was doing. Relationships should be built on trust. So, what were you doing in the forest so close to the city?" Angela asked a little more forcefully. Sam continued to smirk, and he replied, Angie, that is my business, and who said that this is a relationship? Sam's response stunned Angela again, so much so that she nearly stumbled off the building but managed to gain her balance and regain control. "If this is not a relationship then what is it? Angela thought. "I mean we are literally soul mates, who does this guy think he is? Angela decided to speak up, as she climbed to the top of the final building to catch up to Sam, she yelled out angrily, "Hey CAT, who do you think you are?!" Angela approached Sam but noticed a serious look on his face.

"Angie Shh be quiet, get over here quickly, we have a problem!"
Sam demanded. Angela lowered her voice and crawled slowly to
the edge of the building to join Sam on the edge. "What is it what
do you see?" Angela asked softly and a little nervous. "Trouble"
Sam responded seriously. "Look out ahead of you. We are here but
we are not alone" Sam said. Angela gasps and holds her mouth.
"HUNTERS!" said Angela with surprise. "Yes" confirmed Sam,
"And I believe they have my contact" Sam turned to look at
Angela. "I have to go and find him; you stay here this could be
dangerous" As Sam turned to walk away Angela grabbed his tail
and pulled him back. "You are not leaving me here like a helpless
victim, I do not even know what is going on. I can help you, and
since this is not a relationship, I do not need your permission"
Angela said sternly. "Sam smirked at her and said, "but Angie, you
do not even know who you are looking for, if you want to come
with me you need to stay low and quiet, we cannot risk being
caught now." Angela nods her head in agreement and the two
climb down the side of the building.

CAT AND MOUSE

Sam and Angela continue creeping towards the hunters, staying low to avoid detection. "Let's see if we can find out what's going on" Sam whispered to Angela. "There are a lot of hunters gathered here and if we are caught our chances of survival are incredibly low." "I just need to see if they have my friend and then we can get out of here." Sam continued. "Wait Sam" Angela interrupted.

"What if this place has something to do with the missing animals? Honestly, this many hunters in one place are not a coincidence." This may be what we are looking for I think we should find out who oversees this place." Sam was surprised by her analysis but agreed. "There is something strange going on here." They both hid behind an old broken-down car and observed as there seemed to be hunters from all over going inside of a building with various animals. "How do we get inside?" Angela asks quietly.

"Undetected" Sam answered. A black car with tinted windows approached. All the hunters stood still. The car parked and the door opened. "I cannot see him" Angela Said to Sam. "Me either", Sam Answered, "his back is towards us, but everyone seems to be respecting him, and showing him their kills." Angela frowned.

"This is barbaric, people should treat animals with more respect than this, it's sad and I feel ashamed to see them all this way." Sam Looked at Angela with a stern look on him face. "No time for that, once we find out what this place is we are going to destroy it when everyone leaves." Sam said sternly. Angela did not resist the suggestion. Carefully they both watched the stranger give orders to the hunters. "He's looking for something" Angela said, "Yea I noticed" Answered Sam. "He seems to be upset that they cannot find specific species of animals, but what in the world is he trying to do with them." asked Sam to himself. "Wait, look, He's starting to get excited about something, it seems they found something that he was looking for" Angela Said. "Yea and it looks like he and everyone else are going inside. This is just the distraction that we need to get inside." Sam said. "Listen, where is he going"? "I heard one of the guards say that they just got back from the lab on the 37th floor." Said Angela. "Good job Angie lets go". Sam leaps to the side of the building and clings to it with his massive claws. Angela stands in amazement of this unique species of cat, regardless of her situation Angela still has admiration for rare animal species. She admires Sam but doesn't want to admit it.

Following Sam, Angela leaps to the side of the building and follows silently. Sam gets closer to an opening on the 29th floor. There are guards there. Angela holds stills, they both notice the elevator heading towards the 37th floor and pass them. "We must hurry" Sam exclaimed. Sam leaps to the patio of the 29th floor behind one of the guards. With a quick swipe of his tail, he hits the guard in the legs and knocks him in the air, without hesitation Sam leaps in the air towards the guards, grabbing him by the neck and slamming the back of his head to the ground knocking him unconscious. Sam hears a second guard approaching and leaps onto the wall, preparing for a surprise attack. As the guard approaches Sam dives onto the guard crashing him into the ground and knocking him unconscious. Sam turns towards Angela "That is the last of them, come on before they send more guards, we need to catch that elevator." Sam leaps and clings to the wall continuing his climb, Angela is still in awe of what she just saw but knows that she must keep up, so she leaps and follows. "Hey, what was that back there, when did you learn how to do all of that?" Angela asks. "No time for that now, keep moving I'll explain later" said Sam as he speeds up to catch the elevator. Angela Struggles to keep up and Sam starts to pull away, she cannot call out to him, or she may give away their position. Angela notices that the elevator has stopped, but Sam continues to charge forward. "Maybe we should think of a more tactical approach" Angela thinks to herself, but because Sam is so far in front of her, she cannot share her ideas with him until she catches up to him. She attempts to speed up, but Sam is out of her sight now. "Did he already start the infiltration without me?" Sam reaches the elevator floor and climbs inside, there is no sign of Sam or the one in charge. Without Sam's direction Angela is not sure what to do. She realizes how important his directions are, this makes him more mysterious because she does not know where he learned this knowledge and confidence, is it just a part of his species traits? As Angela continues her thoughts she hears a loud crash in a nearby room, she rushes towards the rooms. Throughout the hall she sees guards lying unconscious. "Sam must have been here" She thinks to herself. "Sam Where are you?" She thinks to herself as she continues towards the room in search of her feline partner. When she gets to the room there is a giant hole in the wall and debris all around. Angela enters the room slowly. "Sam." Angela calls out softly. A weakened voice responds to her "Angela, get out of here" Angela looks to her left and she sees Sam laying on the ground, he appears injured but alive. He had only been out of her sight for a few seconds and so much had already happened because she could not keep up with him. Angela knows how to be on guard, she had been trained in self-defense and she attended self-defense classes twice a week. Angela knew she was in a dangerous situation, and she prepared herself as she moved closer towards Sam to assist him. "No, stay back Angela, please just leave me here" Sam continued very weakly. Angela ignored him but prepared herself for what was to come. As Angela got closer to Sam a voice growled out as a warning. "I would listen to him and stay away, you should have left when you had the chance" a voice from behind Angela slowly approach, the hair on Angela's back stood on its ends as the large figure emerged and it resembled a large wolf but standing upright like a man. He appeared to be a hybrid species like Angela herself but instead of being a cat he was K-9, more like wolf. "Your partner seemed to have overestimated his abilities. Maybe you two can sneak around and get past my guards because they are human, but I smelled you the moment you came within range of my nose, I knew you two were watching me from outside, and I have been preparing for you ever since I caught your scent." said the mysterious figure as he fully emerged into view for Angela to see him, the sight of him terrified her. Not only was he a mixture of human and wolf, but he was horribly mutated. "I am Dr. James, Jimmy Brewer, the White Wolf, and you two are trespassing, but more importantly you two are a unique and rare creation. I am curious to how this happened." Angela was still frozen with fear, but Sam had begun to recover. "Stay away from us" Angela demanded. "Oh no Dr. McWaters, you see you and I are much too similar, you must share your secret of how you were able to mere your human DNA with that of this cat." Dr. Jimmy responded. "I have been working closely on this same theory for years and I never knew that there were others out there trying to tame the powers of the animals like I was." Dr, Jimmy continued. "So please tell me how is it that your merger with this animal seems like a success but my experiment didn't go quite so successful as yours appear to be." Angela Stood on her guard, still in awe of everything that she was seeing. She didn't have a clue what this wolf was talking about, but she just wanted to make sure Sam was okay. Dr. Jimmy continued his ranting. "Maybe I should introduce you to my little pet also so that we can compare notes" Dr. Jimmy turns and calls out to someone. "K-9 can you come in here please and meet our new friends. Suddenly a large white wolf walking on all fours emerges from the other room. He seems horribly mutated, and he had no human intelligence at all. He appeared to be a very obedient dog but very ferocious. "Now that the party is all here, I am going to give you one chance to tell me the secret of how you perfectly merged with your host animal, or I will unleash K-9 to finish you and your little cat friend here." Angel stood in fear as she knew he would not believe the story of how her and Sam came to be, she could still barely believe it. None of her self-defense classes prepared her to fight a wolf, what was she to do. Weakly, Sam stood at his feet beside Angela. "You are not ready for this, and I am in no shape to help you, when we have a chance, we need to escape." Sam whispered to Angela. "I agree" said Angela as Dr. Jimmy continued his rant "It's nice to see that you are still alive" said Angela to Sam trying to lighten the mood. Sam recognized what she was trying to do but knew the danger they were in. "Yea, let's try to keep it that way." They both stood ready, weakened and in fear as the large White Wolf Dr. Jimmy Brewer and his Pet K-9

stood blocking the door.

FIGHT OR FLIGHT?

Angela and Sam stood waiting for an opportunity to escape safely, Sam scanned the room for an exit, but the only way out was to climb the walls to the roof. As Dr. Brewer continued to try to convince Angela to join him Sam decided to cause a distraction and allow her a chance to escape. "My sweet dear Dr. McWaters, there is no need to fear me." Dr. Brewer continued. "Can't you see, we have both discovered something amazing here. Together, we could make science history, I have all the equipment, test subjects, and funding you could need to perfect our experiments and perfect human biology to ensure humanity's evolutionary advancement to the next stage. Humanity itself is a species on the path to cause their own self-extinction, my calculations are that humans will be on the verge of extinction if not already extinct before they have an opportunity to evolve into a further developed state of being. We have slowed down our evolutionary process and, in some cases, de-evolved back into an animal state. The modern human has no interest in becoming anything greater than what they have sadly become, which is nothing but mindless consumers. Mindless animals that have no place to fit into the animal's natural order of things. Other species of animals have evolved to live and survive in ways humans could never imagine before. If we learn to bond with our animal brothers and sisters, then we can learn of their secrets and how they survive. We can have access to their natural abilities and resilient bodies. Unlocking the ability of interspecies breeding and the creation of hybrids. Being able to breed with every species on the planet will create millions of different variations of human hybrids greatly increasing our chance of survival and evolutionary advancement. I will blur the lines of what it means to be human and animal, why should a human be defined as a descendant of monkeys? To escape the species curse and evolve humanity into something greater. I want you to join me at this Dr. McWaters. Stand by my side as we transcend humanity and lead the world in the next evolutionary advancement. What do you say, will you join me?" Sam looks at Angela and notices that the look in her eyes means that she is considering his ideas, she seems interested but more important she is distracted. "We need to get out of here and this is the perfect opportunity" Sam thinks to himself. "I need to take advantage of this." Suddenly Sam steps in front of Angela, before Dr. Jimmy Brewer could react Sam had leaped and clawed him in the face across the eye. Dr. Brewer stumbles backways to gain his composure. "NOW! ANGIE GO! GET TO THE HOLE IN THE WALL NEAR THE ROOF, ILL BE RIGHT BEHIND YOU." Yelled Sam as he noticed Dr. White wolf recovering from his surprise attack. Angela snaps out of her thoughts and realizes what's happening. She leaps towards the wall and begins climbing to her escape. "After her you fool!" yells Dr. Brewer to K-9. "I need to buy her some time" thought Sam as he leaps towards K-9 to stop him. "Not so fast little kitty" White Wolf dashed and grabs Sam out of the air. "Damn he is faster than I thought" said Sam to himself as he is forcefully slammed to the ground in his failed attempt to stop K-9. Angela reached the escape hole but looked back to check on Sam, seeing him slammed to the ground in pain. "SAM" Angela screamed. "Just go I'll be fine, get out of here" Sam yelled before being kicked across the room by the White wolf. Angela noticed K-9 leaping on things around the room slowly making his way to her location, White wolf was now looking up towards her also with a very upset but determined look. She knew either she would work with him, or he would experiment on her. "I've got to get out of here" Angela begins crawling along the side of the building making her way to the roof and hoping that Sam will meet her there. "We are in way over our heads" Angela thought to herself. K-9 Finally crashes through the roof, Angela notices and begins climbing faster. K-9 is a dog so he can't climb but he leaps enormous heights for a dog. Angela gets closer to reaching the roof and honestly has no idea what to do if this dog catches her. "Sam where are you, please be okay." K-9 is persistent, even lacking the ability to climb he continues to leap towards Angela. Even at these heights he continues to obey his master at the risk of his own life. "Dogs are so stupid" yelled a voice from beneath Angela, she looked down and to her delight she saw Sam leap out of the hole and speed climbing towards her and K-9. "SAM" yelled Angela with excitement. Sam leaps and grabs K-9 with his hind legs stabbing his claws deep inside his distorted flesh. K-9 yelps in pain as he is pulled out of the air. "You can jump but can you fly you mutt" yelled Sam as he twists and throws K-9 off the side of the building then catches himself with an amazing sliding stop, clawing the side of the building. He watches as K-9 falls and crashes into the ground. He looks up to Angela "Let's go" Angela is frozen with admiration, and she is just watching Sam climb up to her location. "Hey, Angie, are you ok? Let's go, we need to get out of here" Sam command, thinking that Angela is still in shock over the events. Although the day had been a little dramatic, she felt safe with him, but she needed to be able to defend herself now that she knows the kind of things that are out and that she will be facing. They get to the roof safely together. "Now what do we do?" Angela asks rhetorically. "Well, what can we do, is this even our fight to take on." Sam responded. "I know this started as a way to rescue my family, but the situation is so much bigger now." Sam continued. Angela thought and then responded "We tried things your way and it didn't go well, now I have an idea" Sam smiled. "You?" annoyed at how smug he was being "Yes me" responded Angela firmly, I know a guy and I think he can help us. "You know a guy?" Sam said surprisingly. "What guy, how do you know him" Sam continued to investigate jealously. Angela took notice of his jealousy and decided to tease him alone. "Just come on, I trust him, and I know that he can help us" Angela responded trying to be mysterious on purpose and continue the payback for his smug comments all night, now that she knows he cares about her too. She smiled and leaped to the next roof top leading the way into the city. Sam hesitantly follows

but continues to yell out, "Hey what guy, is he human or is he

another cat like me?" Their voices become distant as they both

leap away from the scene. "There are no other cats like you Sam, you are one of a

kind..." Angela responds. In the dark a pair of eyes watch as the two

leap away in victory, leaving him to lick his wound and regroup.

Dr. Brewer growls and drools in anger and frustration as not only

was his offer rejected but he realizes that whatever Angela did to

create Sam he is much more capable and intelligent than anything

he has ever created, and he needs their bodies to experiment and

find out how to perfect his creations.

THE LEADER OF THE PACK

Special agent Mark Jones and his ex-partner John Wagner continue walking down the hall in the secret government facility that John had infiltrated earlier. His partner Agent Jones was able to subdue and capture him but decided to show him what the government had planned to combat the mutant infestation in the city, in exchange he is expecting John to reveal the true source of his abilities. Under observation John was able to perform superhuman feats. His abilities would be useful to Agent Jones for what the government has planned but the two are going to have to learn to trust each other again to work together. John continues to read the files that were given to him by Mark. It's a list of names and people, this appears to be a roster. "Who are these people, Mark?" What is this?" Mark smiled and replied, "it's a list of some of the best people under our program. All of them work with us for various reasons. We help each other accomplish common goals."

"IT SOUNDS LIKE HE IS ABOUT TO OFFER YOU A DEAL, I WONDER WHATS UP HIS SLEEVE." Abraxas said to John. Abraxas is the true reason for how John can do the things he is capable of, but will he reveal this to the government? Can he trust them? John continues to read and is not sure of what to expect but he and Abraxas are ready. The two stops at a closed door. "Looks like a large room," said John. "Wait here while I get the director of operations." Mark said as he walked off. "I SENSE THE PRESENCE OF A SUPERNATURAL LIKE MYSELF" warned Abraxas to John. "Thanks, you are getting better at being a new partner." Said John to himself. "…AND YOU ARE GETTING BETTER AT NOT OBSESSING OVER YOUR LAST PARTNER…" jokes Abraxas continuing a conversation from earlier. Before John could think of a response, there were footsteps approaching, it seemed Mark was returning, but it wasn't Mark. "THIS IS HIM; THIS IS THE ENERGY SOURCE I AM FEELING AND HE IS VERY POWERFUL, BE CAREFUL JOHN." Warns Abraxas again as the two focus on their true reason for the infiltration. "Well, congratulations on your miraculous healing Officer Wagner, you deserve applause for your true sacrifice to this city and to this government. Your presence here has been recognized as a true feat of accomplishment and We accept your application to join the team and work with us again." John looks a little confused but goes along with the story to keep his cover. "That is why you are here isn't Officer Wagner?

continued the approaching figure. "I am Agent Samuel, leader of the Dream World operators, I would like to introduce you to the current recruits." Said Samiel as he walked into view and stood beside John. He had a suspiciously weird smile on his face, the kind you should not trust. "I SENSE HIS ENERGY JOHN; HE IS DANGEROUS AND HE IS NOT HUMAN. BRACE YOURSELF FOR WHATEVER HE IS ABOUT TO SHOW US, YOU DO NOT NEED TO GET TOO EXCITED NOW." Abraxas warns. "You are always this talkative?" teased John to himself. 'I'll be fine, I'm talking to a monster inside of my head and I've been fighting mutants all day, how can it get any weirder." jokes John to Abraxas. "JOHN, HE IS AN ANGEL, IM SURE HE CAN SENSE THE POWER STONE WITHIN YOU, THAT'S WHY HE NEVER ASKED ABOUT YOUR POWERS LIKE YOUR PARTNER DID SO DO NOT HIDE THIS FROM HIM, JUST DO NOT TELL HIM MY NAME AND THAT I AM HERE, WE HAVE HISTORY." said Abraxas sounding cautious. "Wait, we have angels now, like church angels, that stuff was real from sister Mary?" asked john to himself, sounding surprised and a little excited. "…and you have history?" John laughed silently. "YES,

AND IF THEY ARE HERE THEN THE DEMON BROTHERS

CANNOT BE FAR BEHIND. THIS IS GETTING

INTERESTING JOHN; LETS PLAY THIS OUT AND SEE

WHAT HAPPENS NEXT. Samuel continued to smile and as he

reached for the key card to open the door. "Have you been reading

the files John?" Samuel asked rhetorically, "Because I think

everyone would be upset if you didn't remember their names."

Samuel slides the card to open the door.

GOVERNMENT CONTRACTS

The large door slides open, revealing a large training room, inside there are all the people from the files, it seems as if they are all preparing for something. "What is this, some kind of team?" asked John to Samuel. "I was a member of S.W.A.T, I know a tactical unit when I see one" continues John. Samuel just continues to smile. "I'm guessing you want me to join the team or something?" John asks. Samuel continues to walk towards the back of the room, still not responding to John. "WAIT JOHN, I SENSE TENSION, ACKNOWLEDGE THEM OR I THINK THEY WILL ATTACK YOU." warns Abraxas "THEY NEED TO KNOW THAT YOU ARE FRIENDLY" Abraxas continues. John can feel that Abraxas is serious as he can feel himself getting warmer preparing to defend himself. Samuel walked to the back of the room, he stood waiting for John to join him, but the team stood in front. Samuel watches to see what John is going to do. John prepares to defend himself; the team begins to approach slowly. "JOHN, HE GAVE YOU THE ANSWER, YOU NEED TO ACKNOWLEDGE THAT YOU KNOW WHO THEY ARE, HE GAVE YOU THE FILES. WHO ARE THEY?" Abraxas advises. "John begins, "Axel

Summers better known as The Blaze, hot shot news reporter graduated first of his class in medicine but gave up being a medical doctor to pursue a passion chasing action news stories." John continues, "Leyla Jones, inventor of superior sound technology and equipment, contracting with the government for combat training to impress her father." John turns to the next and continues Alex Cabe, the government's lab experiment. Birth defect turned cyborg," "and finally, the alien that hides on earth and waits for humanity to destroy itself, it's silly that we sit and allow you to watch." John concludes. "JOHN, WHAT ARE YOU DOING YOU JUST INSULTED EACH OF THEM" John stood serious now preparing for a fight, "you are the God of Chaos right?" John asks rhetorically. "Are you afraid of these fools, this is a joke, even without my abilities" "I HAVE NO FEAR I COULD EASILY ERADICATE EVERYONE HERE. THE ANGEL AND THE ALIEN ARE THE ONLY TWO BUGS THAT WOULD OFFER ANY CHALLENGE BUT YOUR BODY COULD NOT SURVIVE THAT TYPE OF BATTLE, I WOULD NOT UNDERESTIMATE THEIR ABILITIES." John stood ready for what would happen next, he slowly began charging his hand with nuclear power from Abraxas. The team stood and one by one they stepped aside to allow John passage to the back of the room where Samuel stood waiting. John slowly walked past each of them keeping his guard up but not feeling threatened at all. He continued and no one made a move. "THAT WAS RISKY" warned Abraxas. "I KNOW HOW POWERFUL I AM BUT I HAVE TOLD YOU, NO HUMAN CAN FULLY CONTROL MY POWERS, NOT EVEN YOU WE NEED TO STAY WITHIN YOUR LIMITS." John shrugged, hating the thought of being so powerful but so limited by his body. "I just don't like being bullied; I don't care who it is. I'm not intimidated easily." John continues walking toward the back of the room. Samuel stood, smiling but he was standing beside something. As John approached Samuel, he raised his voice in frustration. "Now what the hell was that? Are you trying to scare me? Don't you know I am an officer?" Scolded John as he continued questioning Samuels Motives. "EASY JOHN, THIS ONE IS NOT LIKE THE OTHERS, HE'S NOT INTIMIDATED OR THREATENED BY YOU. HE SEEMS ENTERTAINED." Samuel finally speaks. "Apologies my friend, this was a necessary test, I was hoping to get an opportunity to see the power stone in action but maybe later?" John is immediately

shocked that he knows about the stone. He hesitates and cannot

speak. "Don't be so surprised, your medical records from the

explosion said there is a large stone buried deep inside of your

head that cannot be removed. That is the true reason you were

released from government service. Your legs had nothing to do

with it, we believed you would eventually die from your wound if

we never told you about it. It seems that you have not only healed

your legs but gained enormous power." Samuel continued as John

stood in shock at the information he was receiving about the truth

on his discharge. "I have heard rumors of the Chaos stone, but I

never believed them to be true I am overjoyed to see what it can

do." Samuel continued to smile as he turned to a large glass

protective case that he was standing beside. "If the rumor is true

the chaos stone can drain people of their life force and they are

never aware of It happening until it is too late." Samuel explained.

You may have possession of the famous chaos stone, but you

cannot control its power." Samuel continued. May I present to you,

your super suit." He presses a button from a remote control in his

hands and the lights inside of the case turn on revealing an orange suit with a helmet. "On the helmet there was a device designed to harness the power of the stone and allow a user to control up to 70 percent of its power when normally without it you can only use 2 percent of the total power. This suit will make you nearly as powerful as a GOD." Samuel continued. "In exchange we need you to sign a government contract for 5 years in a vow to help protect the city and repel the mutant infestation or whatever else the city may face during your enlistment. After your service you will be rewarded your super suit to keep for yourself as appreciation for your service." Samuel continued to smile. "You are not going to be forced into anything, but you and I know without the suit you are as good as dead anyway. No one survives that stone." John stood trying to take in everything that was just told to him. "I HATE TO ADMIT IT JOHN BUT YOU NEED THAT SUIT, IF IT ALLOW YOU THAT MUCH POWER THAT IS ENOUGH TO DESTROY THE VERY PLANET AND DISRUPT THE SOLAR SYSTEM ITSELF. WITH THIS SUIT, IF YOU MAX OUT YOUR POWER THEN YOU ARE GOING TO NEED TO FIND ANOTHER PLANET TO LIVE ON, THIS SHOULD BE PLENTY OF POWER TO ACCOMPLISH OUR

MISSION." Said Abraxas excited to be able to flex his powers a little further if needed. "But what about the 5-year contract? Are you really okay with that?" John asks himself. "5 YEARS TO ME ARE LIKE MERE SECONDS. I AM AN ETERNAL LIFE FORCE I DO NOT CARE ABOUT TIME; ALL I CARE ABOUT IS RELEASING MY POWERS AND BEING FREE. WHY DO YOU CARE? WITHOUT ME YOU ARE BRAIN-DEAD, LEGLESS VEGETABLE? THIS LIFE AND ADVENTURE IS ALL YOU HAVE; YOU ARE STUCK WITH ME AND WE WANT POWER." Explained Abraxas. John thought about it and finally he agreed with Abraxas. "This gives me a chance to be back in the government and protecting its people." John thought as he approached Samuel. So, do we have a deal Mr. Wagner, your partner is waiting for you and the team with your first mission if you are with us." "THEY WERE PREPARING FOR A MISSION; THIS IS PERFECT TO TEST MY ABILITIES." Said Abraxas.

John turns to Samuel, "if this suit does what you say it does then we have a deal, but I'm still not working with a team of misfits like these guys. I'd rather work alone if I have a choice." Samuel continued to smile. "I'm glad you have agreed to work with your government to resolve the current state of this city. Please go put on your suit, we have some action happening in the back of the compound and I need you, soundwave, and Axel to go and see what you can do. Reportedly there are more special ability people there trying to make their way here. Let's give them a hand, shall we?" Excitedly John grabbed the suit and helmet from the case and began walking back to the crew to suit up and battle test before brief of the mission. As John walks away there is a call for Agent Samuel to report to the science lab to meet a visitor. "Agent Samuel, you need to come quickly to the science lab, someone is here to see you and she is asking for you by name, says her name is Angela." Reports to a field agent. Samuel turns to go meet the guest. "I know Angela, she and I are old friends," said Samuel, as he continued to smile.

REVELATIONS II

Samuel continues to walk down the hall towards the science lab, "today is such an eventful day isn't it." He says to himself. To others Samuel is a very suspicious character, he always appears so calm when everything else is in chaos. They do not know that this is exactly the way Samuel likes things, usually, that is exactly how Samuel plans things. Samson and Angela wait patiently in a guarded room. Due to Angela's appearance and Samsons intimidating size, the government agents do not trust her, even with her government I.D. "How well do you know this guy" asks Sam as he paces impatiently back and forth. "We should be tracking this wolf guy…" Sam continues "…we shouldn't be here" Angela notices that Sam is feeling uneasy. "Relax" Angela said. "I've known agent Samuel for a few years now. Occupational relationship. He has always taken interest in my work, and he usually can help me with equipment, or connections to people of the city council." Angela continues. "The only reason I was even out there when you were captured is because I was on a research mission to find out about the effect the water has on animals and why there was a great migration of many animals from the city. In finding this guy I think we can see why the animals are leaving"

"Not to mention the effect the water had on you and me is a direct answer to the effect the water can have on people and animals. We do not want anyone else repeating what happened to us, especially Dr. Wolf." Angela concluded. Sam nodded his head to acknowledge that he understood and wouldn't complain. "Samuel can help us, I know it" Angela mumbled. "I hear approaching footsteps," said Sam. "That's probably him" Angela interrupted as she suddenly started to fix her hair upon anticipation of his arrival. Sam took notice of Angela's attempt to clean herself up for this guy. He was jealous and that was Angela's plan all along. She knew her relationship with Samuel was a little more than complicated and the chemistry would show itself as soon as he entered the room. Angela was attracted to Samson, but he is just a cat and he said that they were only a partnership, Angela did not like that, so she planned to make Samson, a cat, jealous, and it worked. One of the guards slid the door back, Samuel slowly walks into the room, the guard closes the door. Angela turns and sees Samuel, walking towards the center of the room. He has his tactical gear on as if he is preparing for a mission. His signature smile was still planted firmly on his face. "Angie, it been a while since I have seen you, you look a little different" Samuel says sarcastically to Angela as he lifts his arms to embrace her with a hug. Samson leaps off a ledge he had planted himself on to keep from pacing. He lands with a heavy sound next to Angela as she begins to hug Samuel. "And who is this," Samuel says with a smile not intimidated at all from the appearance of the large cat. "My name is Samson, but Angela calls me Sam" Samson responds for himself to Samuel's surprise. "Interesting, you can speak, this is a new one even for me Angela" Samuel says continuing his smile as he finishes his hug and releases Angela to speak. "What happened to you?" Samuel asks curiously "… and it is nice to meet you Samson, I think it's cute because Angela calls me Sam also, something we share in common." Samuel says, looking at Angela. Samson looks over to see Angela Smiling as she begins to reply and answer Samuel's question telling him the story of how the two were merged into one. This makes Samson even more jealous, "I was never this jealous and emotional until I received human intelligence, what a strange burden this is." Samson says to himself. Angela finished her story explaining what she remembers about the incident. "… Now my body is merged with Samson, and I maintain this cat appearance, Samson has gained human intelligence and it appears that our souls are merged into one" Angela concludes her story. "Is there anything that you can do to help." Angela asks. Of course, I will help you Angela, and you could not have come at a better time if I could really use you and Samson, and I have the perfect equipment for both of you.

HISTORY

Samuel encouraged Angela and Sam to follow him further back into the Government facility. "I think I have a way for you to get your human appearance back, well temporarily" Samuel said to Angela as they begin to walk towards the science lab. "Samson, how can I help you?" most of the equipment that we make here is for human use, we do not have any uniforms or equipment designed for a cat to use." Samuel said to Samson. Sam looked at Samuel with a Smug look on his face, "I'm perfectly fine the way I am, I do not need anything from you." Samuel wasn't even listening to Samson, still focusing his attention on Angela. "Your condition isn't too surprising you know." Said Samuel to Angela, "We used to have a specialist who worked with the government, and he was studying the human and hybrid animal possibilities." Angela and Sam Stopped in their tracks. "His name wouldn't happen to be Dr. Jimmy Brewer, is it? asked Angela as she stood still in anticipation to hear his response. Samuel stops and turns around, his smile slightly lowered as he was genuinely surprised at the accuracy of her answer. "Yes, that's exactly his name. We haven't heard from him in years since the committee decided to end his research and terminate our contract with him. He

eventually ran out of funding; how do you know of him?" Samuel

asked, looking even more serious than normal. "Well, we sort of

met him before we came to you." Angela said "He attacked us, he

has transformed himself into a hybrid wolf, he has been

experimenting with numerous animals around the city. He the one

responsible for the hunters." Angela explained. "I see" Samuel said

as he begins explaining the work of Dr. Brewer. "Jimmy was with

the agency before I was here which is a long time ago. We met

before his contract ended as I was becoming an agent." Samuel

continued to explain. Initially he was offered a contract from the

government to help people suffering from organ failure without

having human organ donors". Samuel Explained. "…and how was

he planning to do that" Angela asked curiously. "Well, using

animals of course." Samuel answered. Angela gasped. "don't be so

surprised Angie" Samuel smiled. "It was all in good intentions at

first." Samuel continued. "We were creating animal embryos

containing human cells and then transplanting them into surrogate

animals for the cells to grow" Samuel continued. "The goal was to

produce animals made with human organs that can eventually be transplanted into people." Angela looked confused. "Isn't that impossible?" Angela asked curiously. "Well, most species are evolutionarily distant from us, and only certain species of animals would even work, but basically we are all made from just different combinations of the same stuff." Samuel continued. The government wanted to maintain boundaries between the animals we eat and those we don't, only allowing experiments on animals we do not eat. It became difficult to keep the human cells alive while trying to learn the cross talk between the cells. So, we begin inserting human DNA into animal eggs and then placing the fertilized egg into the human uterus so that natural birth occurred to ensure the organs used were viable to transplanted." Angela turned her head away at hearing such disgusting science. "Even if the intentions were good, you were breeding hybrid to harvest organs, how barbaric." Angela scolded. "Samuel smiled, "remember Angie, I was not here during these times, I introduced a new science to the people. Ultimately, the government agreed with your thinking, and they ended the experiments and the entire project. They ended Dr. Brewer's contract as he was on the breakthrough of the perfect balance, but at this point would it even be moral to sacrifice a functional sentient being to save the life of another?" Samuel said. You see hybrids destabilize our human uniqueness and undermines our moral superiority, so they just cannot be allowed to exist." Samuel said smugly, looking at Samson. They had finally reached their destination, the science room. "We are here, Samson, do you mind waiting outside, the security protocols would never recognize you as a non-mutant. I'm afraid you will be harmed if you enter, I promise I will take good care of Angela and bring her back to you when I'm finished, okay?" Samuel smiled, placed his arm around Angela and walked inside. Samson began pacing, anticipating Angela's return. "I really don't like that guy" Sam Said to himself as he watched the doors close.

CONCLUSIONS

Samuel and Angela walk into the science lab and through the showroom floor where there are numerous specimens and scientific technology on display. They walk down a long hallway and enter a smaller room filled with high-tech gadgets and equipment. "Here we are" Samuel said. He walks over and picks up two wrist bands and then he pulls out a medal cabinet drawer containing a slender body suit. "We designed these to help suppress the animal genes from the human genes in our hybrid creations. Wearing these wrist bands amplifies the technology in the suit, and this suit will suppress any hybrid cells other than human that it encounters." Samuel explained. "What does that mean?" Angela asked curiously. "Well, since you will be wearing the suit the nanites in the material will suppress your cat cells and leave your human cells untouched. This does not harm your cells because we did not want the technology to harm the organs we were trying to harvest." Samuel continued explaining. "It is a low frequency that communicates to the cells and organizes them, so they are attracted to other places in your body. The frequency could also be increased in the event you want to increase your cat cells and abilities." Angela looked slightly excited. "So, I can increase or decrease my abilities at will with this… right?" asks Angela hesitantly, asking if she understood correctly. "Precisely" confirmed Samuel. "The technology was meant to stabilize the cells and maintain longevity. Since your cells are already stabilized this device is simply a way to manipulate your unique condition at will and however you see fit to use it. The technology is safe and approved and it's all yours Angie. Consider it a gift for all the good times we have had over the years. It would be good to see the old you again" Samuel concluded. Angela blushed, "we have business now Samuel, the past is the past let's not go there please." Angela pleaded. "I really want to stop this guy Dr. Brewer and I'm going to need your help if I'm going to do this." Angela places her hand on Samuel's shoulder. "We will always have history, and no one can take that. But for now, I need to try this thing out so that I can get back out there, it seems like you also have other business to attend to. I'll be fine once I'm dressed me, and Sam will see ourselves out." Samuel smile reached and took Angela by the hand from his shoulder, kissed her hand and responded. "I have faith in you Angie, keep me updated on Dr. Brewer he can be dangerous, but we do not need his mutants running around on top of the disaster that is already happening. This suit should help you but stay safe, and when you leave go out the front, there is trouble behind the facility that I need to dispatch agents to handle" Samuel smiles one last time and turns to leave Angela to get dressed. He walks down the long hallways and out the door past Samson. "She will be out in a minute; she has to get dressed." He walks away and Smirks at Samson thinking to himself "Stupid cat" Samson looks confused and upset. "What does he mean get dressed, I know they didn't…" Sam thinks getting upset at the thought of him touching Angie. "I really don't like that guy" as he continues pacing. "Back in the training room John and the others have their battle suits on and their equipment is ready for the mission, all they need is the order to go. Samuel walks back to the battle room. "Is everyone ready to go?" he asks sternly. "There appears to be a heard of mutants attacking a group of civilians as they were heading towards safety. They appear to be trapped and fighting back but they will not last long. This is what we trained for, now is the time to show me your best work as the Dream World Operators." Everyone remained silent and prepared. "ARE YOU READY FOR

THIS?" Abraxas asked. "I'm curious to how much stronger I will be with this suit, so I am impatiently waiting for the GO Order." Answered John to himself. Agent Samuel was finishing his speech. "Good hunting out there, dismissed!" Said Samuel. "THERE IS THE ORDER JOHN LETS GO! WE DO NOT NEED THESE CLOWNS. TAKE IT EASY AT FIRST, I DO NOT WANT TO HURT YOU." John shakes his head in disagreement. I'm done with taking it easy this time I'm turning up." John says as he speeds off to the back of the facility.

RESCUED

Greg and Marcus watched as Josh fell to the ground in exhaustion. Truthfully, they knew they were in no better shape. This has been a very long week, with all the events happening and they still do not have a full understanding of their newfound abilities. They had barely escaped death a few times and they knew their luck would run out soon. At least they have rescued the civilians trapped there so at least they were able to do that, but what do they do now. There is a large horde of mutated civilians heading towards them very aggressively, Marcus has run out of explosives and doesn't have the energy for a physical fight. Greg is tired from his last fight, and he seemed to have used up any power he did have in the fight. He needs to rest and recharge. "Marcus, all we have is our physical training to defend ourselves" Greg says nervously "I'm tired Greg, I have no more weapons and there are hundreds of those things seconds away from us, you want us to fight?" Marcus asked in disagreement. "If we run, we leave Josh and we do not know what they will do if they get him." Greg said as he began to rest. "That's true, but if we fight then we will all be killed or captured" responded Marcus. "Well, what would you have us to do, pray?" asked Greg sarcastically as he prepares to defend himself. "No, I will cause a distraction and allow them to attack me, this suit will offer me protection although I can't fight back much. It may give you a chance to grab Josh and get out of here." Marcus said bravely knowing the weight of his decision. Greg Shook his head, "That's a worse Idea than mines, in my condition I could barely pick him up by myself let alone get very far, let's just hope my powers return during the fight before it's too late." With nothing further to say Marcus turns to face the oncoming Horde with his cousin Greg. "If we go down, we go down together as a family" Marcus thinks to himself as the mutants begin making their way closer to them. "LET'S GO YOU MONSTERS!" "Yelled Marcus as he charges forward towards the heart of mutants and begins attacking. He lands punches, kicks and headbutts but the mutants swarm and surround him. Greg rushes forward to his fate, attempting to save both his brother and cousin but knowing deep down there is nothing he can do. He accepts his fate and charges forward. "MARCUS, JOSH, HERE I COME" Greg Thinks of his wife as he run towards his death. "Cindy, I will see you soon" Aggressively he dives towards the crowd of mutants around Marcus knocks them down and falls to the ground, he is immediately surrounded by mutants clawing away at him as he tries to cover his face. This is it, there is nothing he can do. Pinned down and not able to fight back he feels the claws and teeth ripping away at his flesh. He screams in pain. Marcus hears him but cannot get to him. The mutants have not been able to get Marcus out of his suit yet, but more are on the way. Bigger and some with abilities. The suit buys Marcus more time, but he knows the suit is not indestructible. Greg Continues to scream as the mutant's claw away. "Maybe we should have prayed" Marcus thinks to himself as he hears Greg scream helplessly. Suddenly The mutants turn their attention to something approaching fast, very fast. "NUCLEAR WAVE!" yells John as he arrives just in time by running at speeds exceeding the speed of sound. The combined speed and the forced heat of the blast send hundreds of the mutants flying away and this frees Greg and Marcus, giving them the opportunity to stand to their feet. Marcus rushes to Greg. "Are you okay, what the hell just happened?" I don't know but they seemed to be worried about another threat and not paying us much attention. Now may be a good time to execute your plan of retreat. Let grab Josh and get out of here while they are distracted."

said Greg, "His shirt and pants were severely torn, he was bleeding

from claw marks and teeth bites. He seemed to be in worse

condition and Marcus didn't think they would be able to retreat.

Marcus does not respond but instead looks around to see what has

the mutant's attention. Once again, an orange blur speeds past

them, this time knocking over several mutants, they hear laughter.

"What's going on Greg?" Marcus asks. "It appears that we are not

alone anymore, someone else is attacking the mutants, but who?"

asks Greg rhetorically. "You are really fast John, but I am still

going to take out more mutants than you…" said a woman's voice

from above, Greg and Marcus look up to see a woman glowing and

walking on the air. "SOLAR WAVE" She rains down fire from her

hands and it begins burning the mutants. They begin to scream and

creak in anger and pain. Still larger mutants are approaching.

"Who are they?" said Marcus as he and Greg stands in Awe

watching the mutants fall in defeat to these mystery people. "Hey

Issa, save some for me, go handle the big ones I'll take care of

these little guys," says another woman dressed in military uniform

carrying futuristic looking weapons and an expensive looking power suit. "VIBROACOUSTIC WAVE!!" She yells as she fires a pulsating gun using sound as a weapon. The intense sound forces the mutants to fall to the ground but had no effect on the larger ones. "No worries I'll handle them Leyla" said Issa as she leaps into the air and comes crashing down on one of the larger mutants, defeating him in one attack. Some of the smaller mutants begin to flee and run away as the new threat is more dangerous than the previous. "Oh no you don't" said John as he speeds after the ones trying to escape taking each one down with incredible speed and power. "I CAN GET USED TO THIS" said Abraxas to John. "BEING ABLE TO USE MY POWERS LIKE THIS WITH NO PENALTY IS LIKE BEING ABLE TO FINALLY STRETCH AFTER BEING CRAMPED UP FOR SO LONG IT FEELS GOOD, LETS KILL THEM ALL, LET NO ONE ESCAPE" said Abraxas as John was happy to comply. Issa continues attacking the larger mutants, Leyla continues to fight the smaller mutants that insist on attacking, John is chasing down all the ones trying to escape. Breathing a sigh of relief, Greg sits on the ground to tend to his wounds, he needs medical attention from that attack, and he may need a long recovery if there are any infections. There is fighting going on all around him as more agents appear firing guns and pushing back the mutants. Greg realizes that this is the Government, they are being rescued. As Greg lays down to rest, he hears, "I got you buddy, SOOTHING FLAMES" another government operator walks up to Greg wearing red with glowing hands of fire. "Don't worry this will not hurt at all, ignore how it looks" Axels kneels to help Greg with his wounds but realizes who he is. "Greg is that you?" said Axel. "Summers, what are you doing here" said Greg, confused and pleasantly surprised. Axel and Greg Grew up together and were friends in school before their career took them in two different directions. Axel knew Greg's father and trained with him and his brother. When Greg was busy many times, Axel would be there to help Greg's father before he lost his life on a government mission. Axel was there during the times of Greg's mother depression before she was mysteriously killed. Greg's family had been through a lot, but they sacrificed so much for the city, and Axel was from an adopted home, he never knew his real family, so he was attached to Greg's family. "Stay still" Axel touches Greg with the flames and begins to heal his wound. The heat is comfortable and welcoming, while Greg is healing, he notices that his Gloves are starting to glow with charged energy. "So, I see you found them" Axel says to Greg as he notices the gloves reacting to the power. "What are you talking about?' Asks Greg curiously he notices that Axel has a similar pair of gloves. "What's going on here Axel where did you get those" Greg asks. "Well, your father gave them to me, they belong to your family. I was supposed to protect these until he returned from his mission, and as you know he never did. These Gloves are his creation, all four pairs of them. He was preparing them for you because he knew the family was in danger and it would be attacked one day. He never had a chance to give them to you and your brother, we were still researching all the abilities of each one. When I found out about his death, I joined his unit to continue his research on the gloves until you and Josh were ready for them. That's why I left my Job as a reporter to work for the government. Greg there is a lot we need to catch up on." Axel finished explaining. The mutants were all defeated and killed, very few got away as Marcus and Greg looks at the field of dead mutated bodies that lay all on the ground. Josh had begun to wake up as all the action started to subside. "Josh", said Greg and Marcus collectively, you are awake, are you Okay. "What happened?" Josh asks weakly as he is helped to his feet by Greg and Marcus. "We came to help" Axel says as he steps forward and surprises Josh. "Axel, what are you doing here? It's good to see you?" Josh says weakly. As the smoke and fire settles down, Samuel walks out on the battlefield, a sinical smile on his face. "I will be glad to explain what's going on to everyone." Everyone turns to face Samuel and the members of the dream world team stop their actions and stand ready for orders. "My name is special agent Samuel, I am the leader of this operation and its members, we are here as a part of the Government mission to rid the city of the mutant infestation. We are the Dream World Operators, and we could really use your help Dr. Williams, your family has contributed a lot to this city and your father was a hero for the Government. His death was a tragedy, but we face an even bigger threat than he predicted if we do not counter this infection." Samuel reaches his hand out and helps Greg up, Josh and Marcus stand beside him, the other operators including John stand ready. "Please come back with me to the facility, there I can explain what we do and provide you with proper equipment to handle the mutant threat. I fear something bigger is on its way and we need to be prepared." Greg, Josh, and Marcus look at each other, shrug slightly and follow Samuel and the other back to the facility for a briefing and to prepare for what is to come next. They had barely survived death but for them their adventure is just beginning. "What do they call you Dr. Williams." asked Samuel. Greg smiled at Marcus and said "Awesome Man."

EPILOGUE 1: ZIANE KANDABA THE QUEENIGHT

UNCLAIMED INHERITANCES

As the day ends, there appears to be an interesting turn of events happening. Many of the players are starting to appear, and the story is starting to unfold. They all return home to regroup and prepare for what's coming. The sunlight descends on the city, much of the damage has been done. Those seeking help have realized that there is no help coming. As the sun sets, so do the hopes of a brighter day tomorrow in Green Pond City. In the Surrounding land of Arunika there are still secrets from the past, unhealed wounds creating a dangerous Karma that is only being escalated due to the new events happening. An old soldier returns to a forgotten kingdom with exciting news from the battlefield. The Judgment of Doom, a warrior who stood face to face with the King of the Amaru Army and the leader of the Black Nights themselves, kneels. "My Queen, I have failed." He continued to lower his head in respect and report the events of the evening. "I was successfully able to obtain a living specimen, a host infected with the green water that had not been turned into a mutant, but I was attacked." The Judgments of Doom paused before continuing, slowly raised his head and looked at his queen. "It was a Black

Night…" This got the queen's attention. The Judgement of Doom continued. "His skills and technology were uncanny, his fighting techniques were identical to those that your father used to teach, if I had to guess he was probably Amaru royalty." The queen Stood to her feet; she begins walking towards her kneeling soldier. "You have done well my son." The queen reaches out her hand and lifts the Judgement of Doom encouraging him to stand to his feet. "Shaka, this is great news. That means that the council has reactivated the Amaru and that violates the international treaty signed with our nation." The queen continues to address her son, Shaka, the Judgement of Doom, one of the most capable and trained warriors in her army. "Shaka, we in the Kandaba family are the true Heirs entitled to the wealth and power of the Amaru Family. Years ago, my mother was a servant in the kingdom but married the King of Amaru and they had a Son, my younger brother, Damien. My mother became the queen. Because I was not born of the king and I was already a young child, I was traded to the Kandaba family for secret of the organic metals. These secrets were the direct results in creating the Metal Organic Fibers that the Black Nights are so famously known for. These metals and their secrets belong to the family. My brother and the Amaru clan have been disbanded and report to the council for leadership. Out of respect for the other nations I, Ziane Kandaba, swore on my mother that I would not declare war against the nations for the destruction and death of our people and the theft of its resources. In return the council promised to obtain the resources of the Amaru and divide them fairly among the people, also the Black nights and their technology was to be sold or destroyed forever. The sight of a Black night means that this nation and our people have been deceived once again, but this time I will take back what is rightfully ours, once we have the technology and wealth, we will begin conquering the other lands and become the ultimate power that we were meant to be." Shaka removes his helmet; his face is as serious as his mother's. "Mother, you know this could mean facing your brother in combat, are you prepared to kill him?" Shaka questioned. "Baby brother Damien, a very skilled warrior trained by our father and uncles, the leader and king of the Amaru family, It would be better if he could join our ideals, but if he gets in my way I will reunite him with father and mother, this is our time son, we have been overlooked for too long, the events happening in Green Pond City are just the first sign of things to come, if we are not prepared the mutations will infest our lands also, in order to survive this we need the technology that my father helped develop." Ziane looked at Shaka and held his hand. "Son, we have no choice if we are to survive and bring unity and peace back to the land under the guidance and protection of the Kandaba family." Please go and prepare the soldiers, increase the training, and then give additional rations to the families of the men that volunteer to help their queen with her mission. We will begin growing for the upcoming war, this will be the final stand of the Kandaba family, and we will succeed." Shaka turns to walk away and follows the orders from his queen, he walks to the generals and informs them of her wishes. Ziane retreats into the queen's secret chambers. There is a small door that leads down into the technology chambers of the castle. There Ziane continued her father's work of creating Organic metals. A team of scientists are hard at work creating various protective armor and weapons capable of transformations and containing immense powers. "Is the Queenight Armor ready for action?" Ziane asks her team. "Yes madam, your armor is prepared and ready for deployment" The lead scientist answers. "We need to attack the heart of the Amaru research facility, we need all the information and samples they have available. Due to the orders of the council this priceless information and material are just being wasted and not used. To take on the Government of the Green Pond City we first need the technology of the Amaru and then there will be no Government that can stand in the way of the Kandaba family." The only nation in Arunika with the ability to defeat the Amaru as the co-creators of the organic metals, Kandaba prepares its soldiers for war.

EPILOGUE 2: MASTER ANGEL ZAGZAGEL AND THE ANGEL ARZELL

THE RETURN OF THE NEPHILIM

"The greatest evil in the world does not come from the violation of order, causing chaos, or breaking the rules, but by blindly following rules and never questioning them, by believing that order itself is the divine will of the creators. The general tendency of the universe is to move from order to chaos and then back to order until infinity. Too many rules create a scripted existence and spare you the burden of thinking. Freedom is chaotic. By appealing to so many rules, we are engaging in a war on wisdom. Everything that exists plays an important role in the experience process. Collective learning is the true purpose of consciousness, and there is nothing that oversees that process. An over reliance on rules deprives a being of the opportunity to improvise and learn from improvements. What this ultimately leads to is the destruction of our desire to do the right thing. Please allow me to start in the beginning, let me tell you a story as only I, Zagzagel, was there in the beginning. What I am going to ask you to do is very important Arzell, so you should know the truth before you begin. Understand there are many that are still deceived by legends, myths, and stories. Many still have their biased opinions and they will fight to defend them, you are not to judge anyone Arzell, judgment plants the seeds of self-deception, which in time encourages immoral behavior. I wish it did not have to be you." Zagzagel turns to face the little blue planet called earth as he looks down upon it from the heavens, Arzell kneels before the ancient angel of wisdom, his mentor and teacher of many angels before him, head lowered to show absolute obedience and respect. Zagzagel continues as he walks around his chambers filled with scrolls, writings, laws, and important spiritual scripture that governs and regulates the decisions of countless beings of creation throughout life and eternity. "There are many heavens across many dimensions of space and time. Realities are co-created by the GODS or the highest conscience beings in the scattered heavens. Our heaven is named **Laniakea**, the immense heaven. It is over five hundred (500) million light years across and contains over one hundred (100) quadrillion reality combinations, or universes. The only way that a reality can sustain itself is through balance and not order. The different dimensions are all self-regulating and the creatures in these dimensions are still developing their general awareness of their surroundings therefore, they are easily manipulated. Each creature themselves is a community of living creatures, organized together into individual bodies and ecosystems and are a universe to trillions of living creatures. During the beginning of creation, the governing of all realities was overseen by the natural prince of light, one of the first primordial energies that separated itself to create all the heavens from its body. **Laniakea** is a unique heaven as it was co-created by the four great powers. The prince of light and his brother, the prince of dark energy also the Goddess of time and her sister helped shape this reality. The prince of light took great responsibility of the realities, and he created the angels, the Council of Heaven, his advisors including myself to govern and protect the realities and oversee them from the heavens and the prince of dark and his creatures would help develop the cultures, languages, knowledge, and behavior of the beings in these realities as they develop through time. The prince of light was the rulers of all the heavens and the creative process and the prince of dark ruler of all that is created. All things created has flaws and lacks perfection, the process to perfection is overseen by the prince of dark as the creations are tempted and tested until their virtues are pure enough to enter one of the kingdoms of heaven and contribute to the creation process. Angels, like all creations, are servants to help balance and sustain all realities so that life can persist. There are several things that angels are assigned to do and are responsible for that they never receive praise for. Only creators are worthy of praise and glory, angels are simply servants." Arzell still does not move he knows that his teacher is not being offensive and there is more to learn in listening, angel are servants, and they are pleased to serve. Zagzagel continues. "Everything changed with the creation of the human. Humans were designed to resemble the appearance of heavenly beings, so the prince of light loved them as his special children and even gave them authority over the angels. There was little resentment in the beginning, most angels were happy to serve their new masters. Humans were very unaware of who or what they were and what creation meant. This is where things took a turn for the worse and how we are in our current situation. There was a legion of angels who did not agree with the service to the humans. They took notice that humans had the power to create life and reproduce. This was nothing new to life, but this was the first time a creation resembled the direct design of a heavenly being. Many of the rebellious angels would descend to the earth and attempt to have offspring with the human as an

attempt to control the powers of creation. Unfortunately, they were

successful, and this was the beginning of the first great war in

heaven and the destruction of the unified heavens. The defeated

angels were kicked out of heaven to the dark realm with the prince

of dark to now be servants to the dark prince as demons, used to

temp and test the virtues of humans before they are allowed into

heaven to be the replacement of the fallen themselves. This will

begin the reunification of the heavens. The offspring of the human

and angel hybrid were known on earth as Nephilim. They were

usually mutants and giants, abominations that caused the humans

much torture and pain. There were a rare few Nephilim who were a

successful merger of human and angel, and they were beautiful

creatures, but their intelligence and abilities usually made them

worshipped as GODS. The trajectory of human development

would forever be changed since this happened. Time passed and

humans went through each celestial age, The age of Leo, the age of

Cancer, the age of Gemini, the age of Taurus, the age of Aries, and

now the age of Pisces is coming to an end and the age of Aquarius

is coming for the humans. Much of the Nephillim blood has either died out or is hidden deep inside the DNA of humans that still

carry the cells. Humans seem to be getting back on the

evolutionary track and their consciousness is being elevated. You

can control light and dark energy, along with time and space, many

in heaven consider you an outcast, not human nor angel, a hybrid

species not created by the original creator. Out of everyone in

Laniakea I can trust that you do not have a reason to disrupt the

balance in this reality which could disturb the prince of dark and

the prince of light creating another war between the two brothers.

If this happens this time, the GODS governing the other heavens

will attack Laniakea as a way to balance the heavens peace, then

this will throw balance off in the surrounding solar systems and the

chain effect could destroy this reality. The survival of humanity is

key to the survival of the heavens themselves. We cannot allow

this war to restart. I have information that there are angels trying to

recreate Nephilim. The corruption of humanity has begun, and I

need you to investigate this and bring the person responsible to

face the heavenly council. Be careful, as I have said humans have

evolved and are very powerful, even for an angel like you. Try not

to harm them but know they will not understand your presence.

Those responsible will make themselves known, and when they do

Heaven will be here to assist you. If you are ready stand to your

feet and prepare to depart immediately." Arzell stands and faces

his teacher, the great and wise Zagzagel. "I am prepared to do what

I must, I will not allow the destruction of humanity or the war to

begin, I live to serve." Said Arzell. "Then be off, and report only to

me until we get to the bottom of this thing!" commanded Zagzagel.

With a blaze of fire Arzell flies off to earth to investigate as his

teacher has commanded.

… To be Continued

ABOUT THE AUTHOR

ARZELL the Esoteric (Born Gregory Arzell Willis) is an Atlanta born Native. A military war veteran, serving in the combat mission against terrorism, "Operation Enduring Freedom" in Bagram Afghanistan. Contributor and member of organizations such as the "ACLU", the "HRC", "CARE INTERNATIONAL", "KABOOM!" and the "PTA". Arzell earned a Bachelor of Science in Legal Studies at South University in Savannah, GA and works as a Paralegal writing legal documents for Attorneys. Arzell is a husband, father, and casual gamer. Arzell took an interest in writing after the discovery of historical African American writers, James Baldwin, Langston Hughes, and Dr. John Henrik Clarke. Arzell is a student of spiritual philosophy and various religious beliefs around the world including Christianity, Buddhism, Hindu, and Islamic philosophy, including African beliefs and the Hermetic Philosophy also astronomy and physics. Born on October 31 (Halloween in America) Arzell also takes an interest in occult studies. As an introverted auditory personality type, he is usually alone listening to music to help express his artistic voice.

His writing style reflects a poetic and philosophical insight into life and personal experiences. As a fiction writer he draws inspiration from historical and religious folklore and combines this with science fiction and modern interpretation of familiar stories. So, if you are looking for a poetic and philosophical interpretation of historical and religious folklore in a science fiction universe, written by an introverted African American war veteran, that studies law with Attorneys as a professionally educated paralegal, then you should enjoy Arzell the Esoteric.

9 780578 374628